M000036308

MISEDUCATION
OF A
HUSTLER

The First of a Trilogy

An Epic Novel By
Jabar

PRAISE FROM REVIEWERS

"I like the way the book starts out. This is not your average Urban Novel. There is a lot of build up with all these twists and turns. You really need to read this book!"

-Eatmycookies125/youtube.com

"It's amazing the way that it was done. I like the way this author writes!"

-T.Crosby   Rock Hill, SC

"Already started reading your book… love it and can't wait to chat it up on my show!"

-Donna Walker/Biggchat.com

" I wish I had the whole thing (trilogy) cause that thing is fire!"

-Flyreadz/Youtube.com

"I'm looking for part two. I'm dying to know what happens to Uncle Ronnie!"

-S. Letnom   Milwaukee,WI

MISEDUCATION OF A HUSTLER

Printed in the United States of America

ISBN-13: 978-0-9912174-0-3

ISBN-10: 0991217403

PUBLISHER'S NOTE

This is a work of fiction. Names characters, places and incidents either are the product of the author's imagination or are used fictitiously, and any resemblance to actual persons, living or dead, business establishments, events, or locations is entirely coincidental.

DEDICATIONS

This book is dedicated to the woman who loved me unconditionally and prayed for me when I didn't have enough sense to pray for myself, my late mother. My hearing was impaired by the fruits of the hustle thus many of the jewels she dropped were missed at that time. I hear you loud and clear now ma, thank you, I love you.

To my lovely Queen who has held me down and stood with me through the storms.. I love you.

To my children and nephews who have exceeded all of my expectation, I'm so proud of you all. Continue to follow your dreams, stay humble, and prayed up, I love you. And to my sister, I love you.

ACKNOWLEDGEMENTS

Foremost, God for having mercy on me while showing me everlasting grace. I would like to give thanks to the brothers who encouraged me to write this book, my first. To the haters who allow cages, real or imaginary, to crush their hopes and dreams and wish the same for me, stop wasting wishes, thanks for being my motivation.

To my children's mother's who've done a wonderful job raising them. Lynn whose held strong to the truth when others caved to oppression (you are a Godsend). Vonte who held me down from the beginning (No one can become strong without things like adversity, resistance and problems.), Fly (thanks for leaving no man behind!). Steve Taylor (much love, I understand now), Jerry Brown, Big J (stay diligent we'll be free), Malia (loyalty is all you know, thanks), Smoke (sorry I wasn't there for you R. I. P), Smurf (trust in God, you'll be free soon!), Hardy B (you are always of great help and inspiration, stay on deck our time is coming), Lil Dad (you know what it is, I want for you what I want for myself) and last but not least Darryl Burton (you've inspired much and reached back, much love.) I would also like to acknowledge Rossy (you were one of the first to do it big), Chad AKA J-Bo (one of the realist, you put on for our city!), Max (you've been real since the day I met you, salute), Bally (you did your thing, keep your head up), Fly (one of the loyalist dudes I know), Boo Boo (you paved the way), Pig (the streets miss you, you did it big), Tim Rhodes (always representing the hood), LA (they can't stop a hustler), Anthony Memphis (never seen a sign of weakness in you, you the truth), Lil Tony (wish it was like it was back in the day), Ray (you'll be free in a minute, you know what it is), Money Meech (keep God first, things will work out), Slim (wild ass Slim, you've always kept it 100%), Scotty (times may be challenging but you were bred for this shit, we need more like you), Meech Nun (I respect your hustle, salute), Mike McDowell (never wavering, thanks), Vetto (you've represented,now live well!) Davin (you did it big, keep fighting) and Enoch (against all odds, you kept it real) who stayed true.

This list isn't all inclusive there are more whom I have missed, forgive me it wasn't intentional. My intentions are not to glorify those mentioned but simply to acknowledge them for their efforts in trying to make a better way. We've been the cause of all the calamities for which we've suffered. Our old ways of thinking was the cause of all of our vices and immorality. It is time for us to realize that our acts can be no wiser than our thoughts and our thinking can be no wiser than our understanding.

PREFACE

Ignorance is an evil weed that has held us prisoner far too long. The learned amongst us must educate our peers so that we can remove this evil, no neighborhood can afford to remain this way. The Miseducation of a Hustler series is long overdue.

Questioning things is the beginning of finding the solution.

Jabar.

INTRODUCTION

In the streets of Kinloch the enticement of fast riches are too much for many to ignore. Product is plentiful; you can't live without money so many die or end up doing long stretches trying to catch the ever elusive mighty dollar. This book is a high energy drama that puts you right in the middle of street and prison life.

Many have been brainwashed by such sayings as "The game is cold but fair" but nothing is further from the truth. The knowledge laid out within the covers of this book is for those who have eyes to see and ears to hear. If the reader assumes that this is a how-to book they are truly lost, there is no right way to do wrong.

The Author introduces the reader to Wisdom, Sleeper, Dammoe, Dank and Young Gunner. Wisdom is a boss trying to navigate his way to success, although he understands that the streets are a game of chess where short term tactics are needed for his long term strategy to work, he believes that he can; beating the game.

Together he and his crew come a long way with the guidance of Uncle Ronnie. However, the odds are still stacked against them. This story is sure to hold your attention from beginning to end.

CHAPTER ONE

Dank frantically ran into the apartment out of breath

"Wisdom, Bam and Jinks just robbed Tone from the Horseshoe, he was coming to buy some work" Dank yelled interrupting Wisdom as he sat reading the St. Louis Evening Whirl.

"Where is Tone?" Wisdom asked setting the paper down, giving Dank his undivided attention.

"I took him next door so Sky could bandage up his head. He refused to give up his cash so Bam pistol whipped him" Dank answered.

"I thought them niggas were doing football numbers behind The Walls." Dammoe coughed as he inhaled the Kush.

"They had twenty for drugs, which carries zero percentage on the sentence. Those clowns did eight years because they were fucking up, they should've been home." Wisdom replied contemplating how he would handle the situation.

It was well known that the Boaz projects were separated by four circles allowing each crew to have their own area, thus avoiding conflict. Wisdom and his crew controlled the first circle and ran it like a well-oiled machine.

No pieces were sold there. A few doors up at another one of their spots, pieces, boppers, teenagers, up to half a zip could be purchased. The circle was reserved for those buying zips or better.

His crew was known for having the best prices, so dudes from all over St. Louis came through to comp, knowing that Wisdom always played it fair.

Cake-up and bake-up was in full effect and Wisdom had the game and gone with it. Bricks were going for 24 in the Lou if you knew somebody, if not 28, but in Kinloch if you were good peoples, you could get them for 18.

Wisdom knew that they'd never get rich this way; however they had little choice being that he didn't have a connection. So his crew bought bricks from Fathead for $18,000, turned it into 50 zips, on 26.5 for $850, 28 grams wasn't heard of, and business was booming.

Using a clear flat microwave pan, bricks were broken down to be made into cookies. The trick to the cake-up and bake-up is to add six grams or less of baking soda to each ounce and 1 teaspoon of water for each ounce. Toss it into the microwave, let it jell down, and then stir in the baking soda evenly throughout the work. Remove the pan from the microwave, run some cold water in the sink, and drop the pan in. Once the work has cooled, grab a towel, place it on the floor, bam, you got a cookie.

On hearing this blatant act of disrespect, Sleeper was on his feet, blood boiling. He wouldn't tolerate this, blood would be shed.

"Stand down." Wisdom insisted knowing that reasoning wasn't one of Sleeper's better traits.

"Dank did you tell them that the first circle belonged to us?" Wisdom inquired thinking that these two couldn't have possibly known.

"Of course!" answered Dank

"What did they say?" Wisdom further inquired.

"You young ass niggas don't know how to run a block and ain't no nigga gone stop them from eating." Dank spat.

"Let us prove them wrong." Wisdom said getting to his feet.

"Are they still posted up?" Dammoe asked now on his feet.

"Yes, sitting in the park on the benches." Dank explained.

"Dammoe grab some tools; let's give them a welcome home party." Wisdom said walking into the back room to change clothes.

Dammoe went into the bedroom and came back with an assorted bag of weapons. Wisdom grabbed two blue steel 40 Calibers, Sleeper a Desert Eagle, and Dammoe grabbed the Mack 11. There was a knock on the door, everyone got to their feet ready for whatever. Dank checked the peeped hole.

"It's Sky fine ass." he said opening the door for her. Strolling in looking like a Dime Piece model, Sky commanded everyone attention.

"Hi Wisdom, Tone will be okay. He wanted to use the phone to call his peeps but I wouldn't let him." Sky said flirtatiously.

"Thanks, where is he?" Wisdom asked trying to stay focused but it was hard when dealing with Sky.

"Uncle Ronnie is watching him in my apartment" Sky answered.

"Let's go holler at him." Wisdom suggested. Sky led the way with everyone admiring her hour glass body. Entering Sky's apartment, everyone was shocked to see Uncle Ronnie choking Tone and calling him a spineless Jap.

"Uncle Ronnie what are you doing?" Wisdom asked rushing over to try and save Tone's life.

"Explaining the rules of the game too him." Uncle Ronnie replied, his grip still tight around Tone's neck.

"Looks like you're choking the life out of him." added Sleeper laughing.

"Uncle Ronnie you know that there are no rules in this game, all is fair in war." injected Dammoe.

"Boy, don't disrespect me talking about war. I was in Vietnam; that was a war. What you all call the game was a gentleman's enterprise, with levels of understanding, and respect that you all know nothing about. Not everyone could play the game, it was an exclusive club. But now, anyone can be in it fags, rats, chumps, it doesn't matter. The game is being given too guys, they don't have to earn anything anymore, and that's why it's so fucked up. They didn't have to start from nothing and turn it into something. Someone fronted they soft ass something, now they are in the game, and in the way. He got robbed because his dumb ass was too busy flossing, playing that loud ass music. Had he been paying attention, he would have noticed those two vultures posted up about too have his ass for dinner." Uncle Ronnie spat, anger written all over his face.

"Uncle Ronnie you're right, please let him down." Wisdom requested seeing that Tone would surely be dead any moment. Uncle Ronnie released Tone, dropping him to the floor struggling to breathe.

"Tone, although Uncle Ronnie has a point, I take full responsibility for what goes on in this circle. The quarter bird you were coming to buy, Dank will give it to you but know that we handle all of our business in house; those two will be dealt with. Do you follow what I'm saying?" Wisdom asked making sure that they had an understanding.

"Yea, sure" answered a confused Tone just wanting to get the hell out of Kinloch.

Dank stepped forward handing Tone the work before escorting him outside to his car. While Wisdom reached into his pocket, peeling off five hundred dollar bills handing them to Sky.

"I don't want your money, you know what I want." Sky said in a seductive voice while flashing a smile that could melt any man's heart.

"I got something for you." Sleeper remarked with a smirk on his face that is until Sky wiped it off.

"Boy please, they don't call you Sleeper for nothing according to Pam." Sky shot dismissing him. Everyone busted out laughing as Sleeper stood steaming.

"Sky take the money, I appreciate everything." Wisdom insisted, placing it into her hands.

"Okay, but stop by later." Sky replied seductively.

Meanwhile Bam and Jinks sat on the bench in the park counting the money they took from Tone, oblivious to the consequences for their actions. All in all they got $7700, a chain and watch.

"I'll take the chain and $3000." said Bam handing Jinks the rest.

"Nigga are you crazy? We gone split the money and sell the Jewelry." replied Jinks looking at Bam as if he had finally lost his mind.

"Who are we going to sell it too?" Bam asked knowing that not many people trusted them.

"Aint that Dirty D over there?" Jinks asked pointing in the direction of the basketball court.

"Looks like him." Bam replied, squinting to see who it was.

"Dirty D, Dirty D, let me holler at you." yelled Jinks.

Dirty D was the weed man with money long as Natural Bridge. He didn't mess with the harder drugs because he felt that they brought to many problems and too much time if you got caught.

"You nigga's aint been out two days and you all already making noise!" said Dirty D shaking his head as he approached the table.

"You know how we get down." Bam said smiling as he took a toke from the blunt before passing it to Jinks.

"That wasn't a compliment; you're supposed to be moving without being seen." Dirty D explained although he knew that he was wasting his time.

"Nigga, you do you and we gone do us." said Bam who was now thinking about robbing Dirty D.

"Whatever, what you want Jinks?" Dirty D asked.

"We got this jewelry we trying to sell, you want to buy it?" Jinks asked holding it out to him to see.

"You niggas didn't learn shit in jail. I don't want to buy that, it puts me right in the middle of things, I'm good." said Dirty D not believing how ignorant they were.

"Nigga what are you talking about?" Jinks asked heated.

"Wisdom and his crew aint going to let this ride, dude was one of their customers. If you niggas don't know, murder one is their hobby." Dirty D informed them not believing that they were so careless.

"Nigga fuck them, anybody can get it," Bam spat with murder in his eyes.

As the words left Bam's mouth, Dirty D's eyes got big as three heavily armed masked men dressed in all black walked towards the bench. He began backing up slowly, then he turned running full speed away from the bench.

"What's wrong with that nigga?" Bam said looking at DirtyD like he was crazy.

"BOOOOOOOM," Jinks brains exploded all over Bam's face as the bullet from Sleeper gun ripped off his face, spraying brain particles everywhere.

"He saw death coming." Sleeper answered in a low menacing voice from behind his mask

"Nigga, I'm going to kill you." Bam said reaching for his gun but was stopped in his tracks by Dammoe.

"Don't play yourself, homeboy." Dammoe warned with the inferred locked on Bam's face.

Stepping out of the dark, Wisdom, walked around to the front of the bench to face Bam.

"Fuck you niggas, I ain't begging, yall can go to hell" Bam yelled, spitting on Wisdom.

"BOOOOOOOOOOOOM,BOOOOOOOOM

"You go first." stated Wisdom calmly pulling the trigger striking Bam twice in the forehead with the 40 Caliber killing him instantly.

****

"Do we have any clues as to who murdered these two pieces of shit?" asked Captain Smith walking up to the scene as Bam and Jinks bodies were being taken away.

"No, Captain both of them were just released from prison a few of days ago. This might have something to do with something they did before they went in." Detective Brown answered.

"This happened in the park, there had to be 50 people out and no one saw anything?" Captain Smith asked irritated that such violence was being overlooked.

"Cap. You know how it is around here; everyone minds their own business unless it involves a civilian." Detective Brown informed him.

"What in the fuck are you talking about?" asked Captain Smith

"Cap. These people leave street stuff to street people, as long as innocent bystanders aren't being harmed, they won't get involved." Detective Brown explained.

"So you're saying that two humans can get gunned down in the middle of a public park and no one cares?" asked an irritated Captain Smith.

"These people feel that when a person chooses to live the street life, they know what they are getting themselves into." Detective Brown replied.

"That's some bullshit, Detective Brown, shit rolls downhill keep that in mind." said Captain Smith before walking off.

CHAPTER TWO
(One Year Later)

Drought season was in full affect and Wisdom's crew was eating good. Most people didn't know how to capitalize off the opportunities that come along with the drought. His new connect; a guy from Mexico, told him ahead of time that it was going to be a drought in order to stabilize the market.

This was some bullshit, he knew it. Some greedy Columbian probably wanted to buy one of those new 777 jumbo jets so he's putting a squeeze on the market to pay for it. Can't be mad, its good business, Wisdom thought to himself.

Most people don't realize that the Columbian's cartels keep 25 or 30 tons on deck in the U. S. at all times. These guys are educated in economics so they play on the supply and demand to squeeze everybody. His crew was going to do the same.

"Everyone thought that I was tripping when I started taking a few bricks out of each shipment setting it to the side. We have 54 bricks in the cut. I knew the drought was coming so I wanted to be prepared. Those guys out there flossing will be broke in a month or so because their spending, gambling, and tricking habits won't change. We will capitalize on their short sightedness." Wisdom told his crew.

"How are we going to do that?" ask Sleeper.

"We're not selling any weight." Wisdom answered.

"What?" Dammoe replied sitting up in his sit.

"If someone wants weight, they can buy all the zips they wants for $1000 each, no deals." Wisdom explained.

"We're going to lose all our clientele." said Sleeper not understanding Wisdom's plan.

"We're the only store in town, where else can they shop?" asked Dank with a big smile.

"I'm feeling that." replied Dammoe.

"For everyone else we're selling 5 grams for $250, no shorts." Wisdom explained, looking at everyone.

"Do the numbers, that $50,000-60,000 per brick." Dank said

"I'm feeling that Wisdom." Dammoe said perking up.

"I thought you all would." Wisdom responded

"Y'all going to the car show?" asked Sleeper ready to hit the streets.

"You just want to floss that 442 you just got out the paint shop." Wisdom said smiling at his friend.

"I see he knows you." said Dank smiling himself.

"Yea, but I ain't the only one, you and Dammoe been itching to drop the top on those Chevelle's." Sleeper countered

"No doubt." Dank replied

"Wisdom, what's up with your project? What it's a 62 or 63? Vette?" asked Dammoe

"It's a 58 Corvette; Y'all wouldn't know anything about that." Wisdom said proudly.

"You can only fit one female in it, so it ain't for me." Sleeper said smiling.

"Me either " Dank agreed

All I need is one female." Wisdom said shaking his head at his friends womanizing ways.

"It's all good, Wisdom, you can roll with me" Sleeper offered.

"No good, you keep them lil killers with you, I'll roll with Dammoe." Wisdom told him.

"Why you hating on my lil dudes?" ask Sleeper feeling rejected.

"I don't hate. They're goons not gangsters and their reckless. They think every problem has to be handled physically, instead of using their mental to out maneuver their opponent. It's costing you a small fortune to keep them out of jail." Wisdom stated

"I told you." Dank said laughing.

"Shut up, your pussy bill is costing you a small fortune." spat Sleeper, causing everyone to bust out laughing

"Has anyone seen Young Gunner?" Wisdom inquired.

"He's been hanging out with Uncle Ronnie a lot lately" said Dammoe

"Just what we need, another crazy mother fucker running around here." added Sleeper shaking his head.

"Look who's calling the kettle black." said Dank looking at Sleeper sideways.

Everyone bust out laughing because they all knew that Sleeper was crazy himself, he'd spent a lot of time with Uncle Ronnie, and fears him.

"What time are we going to the car show?" Wisdom asked standing to leave.

"Around 12:30." answered Sleeper

"Cool, I'm going to take a shower; we'll meet back up around 12:00." Wisdom said before walking out the door as Sky was entering hers.

"Wisdom, what's good?" Sky asked with a disappointed look on her face.

Sky is the type of woman that every man lusted for. She was pretty, thick and smart.

"Nothing much." Wisdom answered as he eyed her hourglass body.

"I got something that you can do." Sky stated with a devilish smile.

"Lead the way." Wisdom said admiring her ass as he followed her into the apartment.

Grabbing Wisdom's hand, Sky led him into her bedroom. They began undressing one another, while kissing and caressing each other's body.

Laying sky onto the chaise, Wisdom slowly parted her voluptuous thighs, seeing the fine hairs of her love box starting to become slick, wet; her swollen pussy lips dying to be sucked, licked and loved.

Using two fingers, he delicately began to massage her beautiful and bulbous clit gently, as he spread her legs far and wide.

"I want you so fucking bad Wisdom." Sky moaned

Sky pulled Wisdom head first into luscious pussy. He devoured her, plunging his tongue in and out of her pussy, driving her wild.

"Mmmm, you taste so good!" Wisdom whispered in between licks.

"Oh, yeeeeeees babe, right there." Sky moaned as Wisdom continued to make love to her with his tongue.

"Wisdom, I'm cuuuuuuuuuuuuming." she moaned loudly, releasing her juices into his mouth.

"Kiss me, Wisdom. Let me taste my pussy on your lips." Sky begged grabbing his face into her hands, and slowly kisses him, allowing herself to taste her own sweet nectar on his lips.
Sky was slowly losing her mind as her hands found their way to his dick, which was now completely exposed and at attention.

Softly she tweaked the tip of his dick with her fingertips, bent down slowly and tasted him, placing him into her mouth.

"Shit, Sky, your head game is off the chain." he moaned holding onto the back of her head.

"Thank you for letting me taste your dick. I love to taste it," she said allowing her tongue to slide off the head of his dick before taking it back into her mouth.

"Stand up" ordered Wisdom, she complied, he then backed her up slowly against the wall, licking, kissing, and nibbling his way down her neck to her breasts.

Sucking on her right breast, he began to squeeze and pinch the other as a sweet moan escaped from the back of her throat. The warmth of his tongue sucking on her hard nipples excited her all the more.

Sky's drenched pussy begged to be touched, with his free hand Wisdom rubbed her swollen clit as he continued to suck her breast as another moan of ecstasy escaped her lips.

Tenderly he continued to rub and squeezed her swollen clit before sliding two fingers inside her.

"Damn, babe that feels so damn good." she purred with each delicate stroke.

Rolling her hips Sky worked her pussy on his fingers. Her moans were beginning to grow more as he stroked his fingers deeper in her wetness. Releasing his mouth from her breast, he kissed her lips, sucking on them, as he continued to finger her.

Reaching down, picking her up, Sky wrapped her long legs around his sculpted waist; as his tongue found her wanting mouth. Wrapping his arms around her body, Wisdom elevated her up higher to position her pussy over his dick, and then lowered her slowly onto his manhood; easing his way past her moist pussy lips. Feeling his head entering her, inching its way farther and farther inside her, Sky moaned "Oh, Wisdom I love you."

Wisdom began to bounce Sky up and down on his dick with it all the way inside her, stretching her pussy beyond its limits.

"Ahhhhhhhhh, Ahhhhhhhh." Sky moaned out in pleasure.

"Are you okay? Is everything alright Sky" Wisdom asked slowing his pace.

"Yes, oh yes" she uttered, her arms wrapped around his neck, in pure bliss.

Wisdom continued to kiss and fuck her up against the wall, slowly grinding and pumping his dick into her tight pussy.

"I'm cuuuuuuuuuuuming again." she moaned with Wisdom fucking her straight through her orgasm.

"Mmmm, Yeah fuck me. Fuck me, Wisdom!" Sky whispered with ecstasy in her voice, feeling his dick tickling her navel as their moans and groans grew more intense with pleasure.

He continued to tear her pussy up against the wall for twenty-five minutes, before carrying her back over to the Chaise with his pipe still buried deep inside of her. Pulling his dick out slowly he put her down gently, dick still at full attention and covered with her sweet juices.

"Turn around and bend over," he demanded. Sky obeyed, resting the palms of her hands on the Chaise. Rubbing and squeezed her beautiful ass, he knelt down behind her, ramming his tongue into her pussy.

Sky couldn't remember ever having her pussy eaten so well. Rolling his tongue into a tube, wasting no time, he began licking and darting it in and out of her. With each lick, Sky moaned louder. Grabbing her hips with his strong hands Wisdom tried to prevent her from swaying back and forth as he worked his thick tongue forcefully all over her pussy, causing her to cum three times, as her juices drizzled down her inner thighs, onto his tongue.

Licking her dry before standing, he began stroking his shaft with his right hand while he rubbed and fingered her pussy with his left.

Ready to have him invade her walls again, Sky looked over her shoulders,

"Fuck this sweet pussy, fuck it hard baby." She said arching her back.

Grabbing hold to her hips he spanked his dick on her pussy before penetrating her. Driving his dick in forcefully, she moaned as he quickly found her G-spots with his curved pipe.

Pumping into her slowly, while massaging her clit and increasing his pace, he caught a rhythm. Her ass was in for one hell of a ride. He fucked her little pussy with no mercy grabbing her hips, pulling her up and down on his dick.

"Ohhhhhh shit, Wisdom." she moaned, feeling his balls slamming up against her clit as he pounded and thrust deeper inside her. Whispering his name repeatedly, Wisdom fucked her faster and harder.

Sky's knees began to buckle beneath her, shaking and getting ready to give way. Her extremely intense moans accelerated with each stroke of him inside her better than the previous one.

She could feel sweat trickling down from his body onto her back and being absorbed in her skin. He felt so damn good inside her, tearing her pussy to pieces, slapping her ass, rubbing her nipples, and kissing her back. The more he fucked her, the louder she got. With each thrust of his hips she could feel herself coming to another orgasm.

Sinking into the Chaise they both came in unison. After giving her a few more thrusts, Wisdom collapsed on top of her, breathing heavily from their exploding climaxes. Laying in silence, body and mind numb, Wisdom pulled his pipe out of Sky slowly and asked her "Who's pussy is this?" With as much energy as she could muster, She replied "Yours Wisdom; this pussy is all yours!"

CHAPTER THREE

Rolling off of the Chaise, Wisdom headed for the shower. This was the awkward part of their relationship. Wisdom loved Sky just as much as she loved him; however, he knew that he had to stay focused on business so that his plan could become a reality.

Sky understood Wisdom and his plan but still she wanted more now, the house, kids, trips, and spending more time with him but she knew that she had to support her man in order to have the things she wanted, so she did.

"Are you going to the car show?" Sky asked already knowing the answer.

"I'll see you and your girls there. Wisdom yelled out the bathroom.

"How did he know ... ?" she thought to herself, caught off guard by his response.

"I saw crackhead Willie washing Tracy's car. It was obvious you all were going. She doesn't get her car washed unless she's out trying to catch some wannabe baller" Wisdom said smiling at Sky as he entered the room.

"Do you miss anything?" she asked ogling his body.

"Yes, waking up next to your fine ass every morning." He answered admiring her beautiful body.

"It doesn't have to be that way" she said looking into his eyes.

"In due time," Wisdom said quickly wanting to change the conversation.

"How much longer?" she asked without pressing.

"Not much longer, a few more months." he replied with intentions of keeping his word.

"Great, I can't wait." Sky said smiling thinking about how great it will be.

Throwing on a pair of Polo shorts, Polo shirt, the new Jordan's and his red St. Louis signature fitted hat, Wisdom bent over giving Sky a kiss and smack on the ass before heading towards the door.

"Hey now, you gonna start something you keep doing that." she said smiling

Stepping out of Sky's apartment, Wisdom bumped into Young Gunner coming down the steps. His mother is a drug addict and his father is doing life for a string of robberies commit while strung out.

Wisdom had taken a liking to Young Gunner and started letting him hang around but it was Uncle Ronnie who took a liking to him the most.

Knowing that Young Gunner would learn a lot from Uncle Ronnie, Wisdom encouraged the relationship. Uncle Ronnie isn't any of their uncles. Wisdom's mother died when he was 12 and he was soon thereafter placed in the custody of the Division of Family Services but ran away, living wherever he could in Kinloch.

Dammoe and Sleeper's mothers were sisters strung out on drugs living in Las Vegas. They lived with their aunt and her abusive boyfriend since they were 11 and 12, whose only concern was getting the check from the State each month.

Dank lived next door to Uncle Ronnie and fell in with Wisdom, Dammoe and Sleeper when he was 8. Uncle Ronnie took them in, treating them like family after learning that they were living on the streets. During this time he taught them survival skills he'd learned in Vietnam and helped them better understand the streets.

Uncle Ronnie had never been in the game; however, he quickly began to observe the mistakes being made while grasping a better understanding of why young men got locked or killed. These things he tried to impart on the boys but not everything he taught was retained or put to use.

The first and most important lesson he taught them covered the law, which most street hustler were ignorant too. You see, Uncle Ronnie had a run in with the law himself while in Vietnam; he allegedly shot his Sergeants while out in the field.

Although they couldn't prove it was him, he was placed in the brigs and charged with the shooting. The Army gave him a youngster lawyer fresh out of law school who didn't know shit. So he began studying the law himself, helping to prepare his defense. After 10 months in the brigs, with no new evidence, the charges were dropped, and he was given an honorable discharge because they couldn't prove it was him.

If they had CSI back then, Uncle Ronnie's ass would still be locked to the board.

"Do you know who Miranda, RICO, Dana, or CCE are?" Uncle Ronnie asked looking at all of us as we sat at the kitchen table.

"Who?" asked Sleeper who had no idea of what Uncle Ronnie was talking about.

"No," answered Wisdom who was equally lost.

"Naw," said Dammoe

"How are you going to play a game if you don't even know the rules? When the police tell you that you have the right to remain silent and that anything that you say can and will be used against you, is called a Miranda warning established by the U. S Supreme Court in Miranda v. Arizona." Uncle Ronnie schooled them.

"What if the police ask your name?" asked Sleeper

"The law requires that you provide your first name, nothing else." Uncle Ronnie answered reaching into his pocket, pulling out four business cards that read: Jason Rockford, Attorney at law.

"Remember if the police have you, they already know your name, give them this card. Tell them that you are invoking your Fifth Amendment Right to remain silent. I don't care if they beat the shit out of you, don't say anything. Second, and most importantly, if they are asking question, then they don't already know the answer." Uncle Ronnie said looking at them making sure that they understood him.

"What you're saying makes sense." replied Wisdom who'd never given the law much thought besides staying out of their way.

"Now the RICO Act was created because the government wanted a way to go after the mafia in a catch all scheme. There are several predicates which must be met before you are to be charged and convicted with the RICO Act. You all need to be aware of the predicates." advised Uncle Ronnie

"Are you telling us that it's not wise to have an organization?" Wisdom inquired.

"What I'm saying is you must educate yourself in whatever business you are going to get involved in. If you wanted to be a doctor you would go to school for that profession. Therefore if you are going to be in the streets, you need to understand the law. Basically what I'm saying is, if you all have an organization, make sure that the predicates of RICO aren't present in your organization. Now, the Dana that I'm referring to is DNA. DNA is easily left behind so you must be beyond careful when you're doing anything; I will teach you more about that later. Finally, the CCE which is also known as Continuing Criminal Enterprise. This is another catch all law that a lot of brother's fall victim too, you need to understand those predicates too." Uncle Ronnie further educated them.

"We need to hit the books." Wisdom replied not realizing how much he didn't know.

"You do, bending the rules takes calculated thought and leads to no repercussion; breaking the rules only requires reckless disregard and is punishable by death. Big corporations bend the law all the time because they have teams of lawyers who know how to bend the hell out of it without breaking them" Uncle Ronnie stressed.

"Is that why we have Mr. Rockford?" Dammoe asked

"Yes but he is only as good as you are, that's why knowing the law is so important. Mr. Rockford isn't a magician, he can't make evidence disappear." Uncle Ronnie said hoping that he was making himself perfectly clear.

"Whatcha mean?" asked Sleeper confused.

"I mean if you leave DNA, go in there and confess, and give them the gun. You've made his job that much easier and your chances of winning that much slimmer." answered Uncle Ronnie

"Makes sense." said Sleeper thinking that what Uncle Ronnie was saying was common sense.

"Sleeper, common sense ain't so common. Don't assume that you know something; do your due diligence, so that you don't make a mistake that will cost you your freedom or your life." Uncle Ronnie emphasized.

"Yes, sir." Sleeper said now realizing that he was being cocky.

"I love you boys. I will teach and support you; however, I don't support ratting on any level i.e. flat out ratting or dry snitching. When a man makes a conscience decision to play the game and enjoy its fruits, he should be able to live with the consequences that come along with it." Uncle Ronnie said looking into each of their eyes

"Dank, you haven't said anything." Uncle Ronnie said causing Dank to put his pen down.

"I'm taking notes Uncle Ronnie. I read somewhere that if people would spend 30% of their time working 30% of it learning, 30% of it sleeping, then they would only use 10 of their time to talk which would probably save a lot of people's lives ." Dank answered

"Great answer." replied Uncle Ronnie impressed with Dank. Snapping out of his thoughts, Wisdom smiled as he noticed how Young Gunner's body was filling out from the running and daily workouts Uncle Ronnie has him doing.

"What's good youngin?" Wisdom asked giving him a pound.

"You know what it is Wisdom, just trying to get ready for when I'm called up to bat. Got to make the family look good." answered Young Gunner smiling.

"You're already making the family look good by going to school and staying out of trouble." Wisdom explained.

"Yea but you know I love the block." Young Gunner replied with pride in his eyes.

"The streets don't have any love for any of us youngin, don't you ever forget that. We're trying to get this money so we can get out of the streets, you feel me?" Wisdom asked with a serious look on his face.

"No doubt," Young Gunner answered. His respect for Wisdom was written all over his face.

"Dammoe and I are on our way to the car show, you want to go?" Wisdom asked already knowing the answer

"Hell yea!" said an excited Young Gunner.

"Go put your burner up, there's Dammoe."
Wisdom said nodding his head at Dammoe entering
the circle. Then he noticed the frown on Young
Gunner's face.

"What's wrong?" Wisdom questioned.

"You know I keep the toaster, warm in the
holster. I ain't going nowhere without it," Young
Gunner answered standing his ground.

Wisdom had to smile but realized that Younger
Gunner slept on him.

"Go put it up, I got you" Wisdom told him.
Dammoe, pulled up in his 1972 drop top Chevelle; Sky
blue with dark blue interior, dark blue rag top, dark
blue racing stripes, sitting on some 22" chrome shoes.

"Damn this deal is hot." said Young Gunner
excitedly.

"No doubt youngin. Finish school and it's
yours." Dammoe told him.

"Don't be bullshitting me," shot Young Gunner
with a serious look on his face.

"I would never do that," replied Dammoe
Wisdom road shotgun with Young Gunner sitting
behind him. Before Dammoe could pull off Young
Gunner tapped Wisdom on the shoulder.

"What's up with my toaster?" he asked
Wisdom, hit a couple of button on the radio, a secret
compartment opened between the bucket seats
revealing three 40. Glocks.

"Damn, that's some James Bond shit." said
Young Gunner impressed.

"I told you I had you youngin." Wisdom replied
smiling.

Leaving out of Kinloch, they looked like a mobile car show with Dammoe leading the pack. Followed up back Dank in his 1972; drop top platinum Chevelle with the black rag top, black interior, black racing stripes and chrome shoes. Sleeper brought up the rear with his 1970; drop top 442 that's burnt orange, with the black rag top, black interior, black racing stripes and chrome shoes.

The car show was being held at the Review Circle; Dude throwing it owns one of the hottest car shops in the Lou and represents to the fullest. Rappers out in LA are shouting him out in songs. Right now, Ole boy shitting on the game with platinum Acura NSX.

"Stop at the Liquor Doctor and grab some Hennessey and Remy Martin VSOP." said Wisdom as they rode down Jefferson.

"That's what I'm talking about" said Young Gunner rubbing his hands together.

"You ain't drinking." Dammoe informed him.

"Shitting me!" yelled Young Gunner

"Fall back youngin, who's gone protect the family? We need you to be on point." Wisdom said which calmed him down. This put a smile on Young Gunners face. He always wanted to be a part of a family and to know that they needed him felt good.

The Liquor Doctor's lot was packed, everyone trying to get some liquor or ice before hitting the car show.

"Damn who stunting like that?" asked Young Gunner seeing the chameleon color Range Rover hit

the lot, followed by a white Lexus Truck, a 6 series
EMX, and a drop top Viper.

Box pulled up jumped out of the Range Rover,
giving Wisdom a nod of respect which Wisdom
returned.

"Young Gunner, you need to understand
something. Just because a dude shining doesn't mean
he papered up." Wisdom schooled him.

"Whatcha mean?" asked Young Gunner

"Those guys are living off fronts." said Wisdom
turning to look at him.

"You mean they're workers?" ask Young Gunner
surprised.

"Yep," Wisdom replied

"We need to be working for whoever they
working for" Young Gunner was saying when Sleeper
approached the car.

"What?" asked Sleeper snapping on Young
Gunner causing him to reach for his toaster that he
didn't have.

"Sleeper, educate him." said Wisdom turning
back around in his seat.

"We don't work for nobody, everything we got
we earned and it's paid for. If we wanted to go buy 20
Range Rovers it wouldn't be a problem but the feds
would be all over us." Said Sleeper mugging him.

"Young Gunner," Wisdom callout over his
shoulder."Don't ever reach for your toaster like that
again, we're all family. You understand?" Wisdom
asked now turning around looking him dead in his eyes.

"Yes" answered Young Gunner.

CHAPTER FOUR
(What Part of the game is this?)

"Wisdom Jones you were found guilty by a jury of your peers of two counts of first degree murder." said Judge Roper looking over his rimless glass, at wisdom.

"Would you like to make a statement Mr. Jones?" Judge Roper inquired.

With a menacing smile Wisdom told the Judge

"No matter how deep and dark the dungeon you throw me in, no matter how bad the circumstances. I will take my lumps, guard my reputation, and walk away bruised but nowhere near broken. A valuable lesson has been carved into my heart. I vow to never allow it to happen again." Wisdom said looking the Judge Roper in the eye as the audience cheered and applauded his statement. Judge Roper became red as a beet, banging his gavel.

"Order, Order,"

"One more outburst like that and I'll clear the courtroom." he declared.

"Mr. Rockford, do you have anything to say?" asked Judge Reed.

"Yes, we reserve our right to appeal." Mr. Rockford replied handing the Judge a Notice of Appeal.

"So noted, Mr. Jones on the 21st day on June 2008, you are sentenced to two consecutive terms of life without the possibility of probation or parole. May

God have mercy on your soul." said Judge Roper
before banging his gavel indicating that sentencing was
over.

"I'll fight this until I get you out, stay out of
trouble, and don't give up." Mr. Rockford whispered
into Wisdom's ear.

"I hear yea." Wisdom replied.
The Sheriff handcuffed Wisdom preparing to escort
him from the courtroom; stopping in front of Sky who
was crying.

"Sky, move on with your life. Take the money
you have saved and follow your dreams." Wisdom
whispered before walking off as Sky began to sob
harder.

Sky's cries were deeper then Wisdom knew,
knowing that Wisdom was fighting for his life, she'd
never found the right time to tell him about his
daughter; Justice Jones.

Uncle Ronnie, Dammoe, Dank, Sleeper, and
Young Gunner were all present, on their feet, ready to
go to war. Until Wisdom mouthed the words "Stand
down" as he was led out the door to the awaiting gray
goose that would take him to the Jefferson City
Correction Center also known as "The Walls" to begin
a fight that he knew nothing about.

****

The long ride gave him a lot of time to reflect on
his life and the mistakes he'd made, all in an attempt to
escape the hood.

After two long hours the bus pulled up to The Walls, at first glance, Wisdom couldn't help but notice it's resemblance to the prison in Shaw Shank Redemption.

Stepping off the bus, he was led into H-Hall, an old, cold, creepy building used to house intake and clothing exchange. The first thing he noticed was a sign that hung above it "Leave All of Your Hopes, Wishes and Dreams Behind."

That doesn't apply to me, Wisdom thought, as he walked under it; I'm getting out of this living hell, he whispered to himself. Snapping him out of his thoughts was the voice of someone trying to get his attention.

"Strip off all your clothing and throw them in a pile over there." Instructed the huge guard, Wisdom complied.

"Lift your hands in the air, open your mouth, run your fingers through your hair, wisdom complied.

"Turn around and show me the bottom of your feet." Wisdom complied.

"Now bend over at the waist, spread your cheeks and cough!" Came the guard's final instruction but Wisdom just stood there looking at him.

"Hold up, what part of the game is this?" Wisdom asked now feeling not only disrespected by degraded by such a request.

"Everyone has to go through this. Don't make it more complicated than it has to be." said a big corn fed guard. Reluctantly Wisdom complied, and then quickly grabbed his things walking over to clothing exchange.

"What size shoes do you wear?" ask the older inmate behind the counter.

"They're your size!" Wisdom spat quickly getting into a fighting stance. The older inmate burst out laughing making Wisdom feel a little bit stupid. Pointing at the sign, he explained to Wisdom that this was intake were clothing, bedding, shoes, and bath towels were issued.

Wisdom felt a little embarrassed but knew that he needed to be prepared for anything in this place.

"So what size shoe do you wear?" asked the older inmate again.

"8 1/2 shoes, 32-30 pants, 2x shirts." Wisdom ran off his measurements.

The older inmate came back with a bundle of items for Wisdom. Trying on the boots, they fit but the pants didn't. Assuming that the older inmate had made a mistake, Wisdom gave him his size again.

"Young man, this ain't Frontenac Mall, one size fits all. When you get to the hill see Benny, the tailor. He'll tailor everything for you for a couple packs of Kools. Where are you from?" asked the older inmate.

"Kinloch," replied Wisdom with pride in his voice.

"You have several homeboys on the hill, they live in 3 house. By the way they call me Doc, if there's anything that you need that your homeboys don't already have on lock, holler at me." said Doc.

"Ok, Wisdom replied just to move things along.

"What they call you?" ask Doc

"Wisdom," he replied

"Okay, Wisdom, grab your things and head down that hall, make a left, and see the guard at the desk." said Doc

Grabbing his things, Wisdom, followed Doc's directions, arriving at the guard's station, where he encountered a heated conversation between the guard and another inmate. Stepping back to give them their privacy, Wisdom approached when it appeared the conversation was over.

"Wisdom Jones, I was told to report to you." Wisdom said as the other inmate stood looking on.

"I know who you are; you're being assigned to 3 house, 8 walk, cell 209. Why you still standing there, you need an escort?" spat Officer Brown

"Watch your mouth." Wisdom warned knowing that how you begin something was how you ended it and he wasn't about to let these hillbillies start talking to him any type of way.

"I'm Man-Man follow me," stated the inmate who'd just been arguing with the guard.
Wisdom stood there looking at him like he was crazy.

"Oh, you don't remember me, ha-ha? I'm Diamond's big brother; we lived up by the high school in Kinloch. You went to school with my two lil sisters." Man-Man explained.

"Yea, I remember you, damn; you've gotten big as hell." said Wisdom looking at all of the muscles bulging from places that Wisdom didn't know that you could have muscles.

"Yea, prison can do a body good, if you stay away from the wrong things." said Man- Man before walking towards the door as Wisdom followed.

With the door open, Man-Man stopped; turned and told Officer Brown

"Greed causes a man to do a lot of stupid things, don't be one of those men," then stepped into the prison yard.

Man-Man led Wisdom across the yard pointing out what was what and who was who. He explained that the prison was divided by neighborhoods, gangs, and religious sects.

"You have the crips, bloods, GO's and a few Vice Lords but everybody really repping their city. Northside and Westside still don't like each other but stay out of one another way. Southside niggas off the Dark are holding their own and don't click with nobody. Niggas from Pinelawn and Wellston are riding together. There are six of us from Kinloch on the hill and a couple of lames from out our way in the hole. Berkely is like family so we consider them hood. For the most part Wisdom, prison is about respect and minding your own business." Man-Man said stopping to look Wisdom in the eye making sure that he understood him.

"I got you." Wisdom assured him

"Don't sleep on anyone" Man-Man explained. "Most prison murders are committed by fags. A lot of guys assume that they are soft because of their sexual preference."

"Fags?" questioned Wisdom with a puzzled look on his face.

"If a nigga will fuck with a dick, he's dangerous and suicidal. Regardless of their sexual preference, never forget that he's still a man." Man-Man emphasized.

"Fags," Wisdom repeated to himself still not completing understanding the logic.

Entering 3 house which seem like a city within a city, Wisdom looked up to see guys leaning over the rails talking, passing items, while others gambled.

"Come on, we live at the top on 8 walk." said Man-Man leading the way. Looking around on their way up, Wisdom couldn't help but notice there weren't any guards anywhere around. Noticing his questioning eyes Man-Man said "convicts run everything around here."

Reaching 8 walk, Man-Man stopped at cell 201 were Big Hands lived. He was one of the guys off the block whose understanding wasn't all that good. I guess you would call him a goon's goon. He lives by himself because no one else can get along with him.

"Big Hands this is Wisdom." Man-Man said making the introduction.

Rising from his bunk, Wisdom was amazed that the 6'8, 300 behemoth could fit in such a small cell. Reaching inside of his mattress, Big Hands came out with a poker about six inches long.

"Here, Man-Man will show you where to hide it," he said handing the knife through the bar to Wisdom before returning to his bunk to watch television. Looking at the knife, Wisdom couldn't help but wonder how many bodies Big Hands had caught with it.

"Thanks." replied Wisdom at least he thought.

Moving down the walk, Man-Man stopped at Cell 203, Rain and Brinks were playing Chess. Not wanting to break their concentration, they stood quietly at the door observing the board.

"Who's going to win this game Wisdom?" Brinks asked without looking up from the board. This caught Wisdom by surprise, how did he even know his name, he thought to himself. Looking over the board, considering all the possibilities, Wisdom quickly realized that he was in a quagmire. The only pieces left were Brinks' black Queen on B-1 and his King on C-1. Rain's King was on C-3 and his Queen was on D-3.

"It'll be a draw. Wisdom answered

"A draw? I'm about to checkmate his ass." yelled Rain...

"May I ?" Wisdom asked looking at Brinks

"Please do," replied Brinks

Steeping over to the board, Wisdom moved Brinks Queen from B1 to 83 putting Rain in check. Rain quickly captured Brinks Queen with his Kings, smiling thinking that Wisdom had made a major blunder, and then it hit him.

"You tricked me." said Rain

"Naw, your over confidence prevented you from considering all of the possibilities." informed Wisdom stepping back over to the door.

Brinks and Rain were not only old hustlers but cousins. Brinks got his name because he pulled off the biggest Brinks heist ever; and they never found a dime of the money.

As the story goes Brinks figured out a way to get into the Brink's building without ever being noticed. Although the Brink's Corporation was making tons of money, they were extremely cheap. Their depot, located on the corner building of a strip mall, was their weak spot. Brinks saw an opportunity when the DMV moved its office which was next door. Bricks secured a lease for his dummy company, Easy Insurance, preparing to snatch the bird's nest that was on the ground.

His investigation revealed that there was only one person at the depot during the grave yard shift, so he planned to strike then. Removing the drywall from the bathroom which was connected to the bathroom in the depot, Brinks quickly and quietly snuck in, catching the guard asleep, after tying him up, Brinks made trips all night loading bags of money into his waiting truck. It was reported to be $21 million in untraceable cash.

The feds wouldn't touch the case because there wasn't any real evidence linking Brinks to the robbery but the state wanted him. Brinks was tried and convicted because they found one of his finger prints in the rented building and given 30 years.

Brinks has been down 18 years, since 1990 but they keep denying him parole. They've offered to let him out if he told where the money was, he continues to proclaim his innocence.

Rain got nabbed in 1992. He started out in the game selling spoons of weed, moved up to Tee's and Blues, and got in early on the cocaine trade.

His connection out of Florida was giving him uncut bricks for $10,000 Rain would bring them back to Kinloch selling them wholesale for $24,000, life couldn't be better.

With money came lots of jealously. Rain bought a nice house in Chesterfield, a new Benz, a Corvette, and a Blazer for himself. His wife drove a Jaguar.

On any given night, Rain could be found in the Cotton Club buying drinks and talking shit. His world came crashing down when a guy tried to rob him in the parking lot of the Cotton Club, when Rain unloaded a full clip in him.

The jury rejected his claim of self-defense, finding him guilty of second degree murder; he received life with parole because the prosecution argued that it was an over kill.

The law requires that Rain do 15 years before becoming eligible for parole. He saw the board a year prior but got a 5 year set back.

"Who taught you how to play Chess?" Brinks inquired, impressed with Wisdom game

"Uncle Ronnie." Wisdom quickly replied. This revelation startled Brinks and everyone noticed.

"Is there something wrong?" asked Wisdom now feeling a bit uncomfortable.

"No, no, it's just been a long time since I heard that name." answered Brinks composing himself.

"Do you know him?" Wisdom questioned, wanting to know more.

"Yes, I do, we were close." Brinks answered

"Are you guys beefing?" ask Wisdom

"Nothing like that, we just grew apart." said Brinks with a weak smile. Noticing how uncomfortable

the conversation was getting, Man-Man tapped
Wisdom on the arm indicating that they need to go.

"We'll catch up with yall on the handball court
tonight." said Rain as they were leaving out the door.

"Cool." replied Man-Man before heading down
the walk reaching what would be Wisdom's cell until he
could figure out how to get out this cage.

Man-Man yelled "Rack 209."
Stepping in Wisdom was shocked to see how organized
the place was.

"You're on the top bunk." Man-Man told him.

"Who lives on the Bottom?" Wisdom wanted to
know.

"Jamaal, he's from the hood and works down the
hill at the license plate factory." said Man-Man

"I thought yall had things on lock. Why does he
work?" Wisdom asked.

"Because everybody jails different but ask him."
said Man-Man

"O'yea what am I supposed to do with this
knife?" asked Wisdom holding it up.

"It's better to have and not need, then need and
not have." answered Man-Man

"Makes sense." said Wisdom looking at the knife
in his hands.

"I have a few things that I need to go check on.
Get your things together and we'll walk to chow
together when they call mainline. You can meet Wink
then." said Man-Man before stepping out of the cell
closing the gate behind him.

After making his bunk and tucking his things away Wisdom jumped onto his bunk using the time to think before his celly got off work.

On reflection wisdom realized that he had nothing which he could compare this place; he had never visited nor even heard of a place this crazy.

It took a couple hours but he regained self-control enough at any rate for his mind to begin functioning. He began wondering if this was something you might call Karma for all of the things he had gotten away with.

Wisdom never considered himself an unlucky person, for the simple reason that he'd been blessed in all he did. It was not that he had avoided the system only that it had never become so apparent a reality until today. Going to trial, being found guilty and sentenced is one thing. Being locked in one of these small cages is quite another, reality comes sooner than later.

CHAPTER FIVE

Wisdom found himself not so much bemused as curious. Why had this happened to me? Who orchestrate this? Those were the questions he had to answer, lest it happen again.

He'd never known immediate fear in his life but nothing could have prepared him for this; his life taken from him with malice intent. But he was hell bent on getting it back.

Wisdom knew from his years of teaching from Uncle Ronnie that he needed a plan. His first order of business was getting a job in the prison's law library. He figured if the law got him here, then it could get him out.

"MAAAAAAAAAAINLIIIIIIIIINE," someone yelled and then all of the cell doors were opened. Posting up at the door, Wisdom waited on Man-Man to walk by but instead was met by Brinks.

"Man-Man had something to do, we can walk down together. Usually we don't eat in the chow hall. We have guys that work on the docks in the kitchen that bring us anything we order which allows us to cook in the cell." Brinks told him.

"What's wrong with the chow hall?" Wisdom asked.

"You'll see. Wisdom it is important that you understand that this place is an animal factory. Logic and reason doesn't govern anything in here. Most of the guys don't understand anything but cold steel." Brinks further educated Wisdom knowing first hand that that knowledge, wisdom and understanding gained by experience, was of inestimable value.

"Sounds like the streets." Wisdom replied after giving what Brinks had said some thought.

"There one and the same. Instead of coming in here educating themselves in the law, business, or economics, precious time is wasted chasing baller fantasies, blaming others; the white man, self-pity, schemes, fags or drugs." Brinks said shaking his head.

"Change isn't easy." Wisdom countered Stopping dead in his tracks, Brinks grabbed Wisdom by the arm pulling him to the side.

"Wisdom, there are two great rules in life, the one general and the other particular. The first is that with will and drive a man can achieve anything in life he desires only if he tries. The particular rule is that every individual is more or less of an exception to the general rule." Brinks said before releasing him.

"Huh?" said Wisdom

"These places are not designed for rehabilitation." Brinks continued.

"But they offer classes." Wisdom injected.

"Classes that offer general information that give the appearance of opportunity so that they can continue to obtain federal funding. Brinks spat

"So how does a man change?" Wisdom inquired.

"Once a man determines that he has a mission in life, that it's not going to be accomplished without a great deal of sacrifice and maybe some pain, and that the rewards in the end may or may not outweigh the pain then when it comes, he will survive it." Brinks said

"That doesn't sound easy." Wisdom admitted

"Nothing in life worth having is." said Brinks as they entered the chow hall.

Looking around, Wisdom couldn't believe how big the chow hall was, there had to be at least 500 people in there. He quickly noticed that it was divided in sections with the whites and squares sitting closer to the door. The Mexican and Indians sitting close to the whites. The Muslims, Moe's, and Nation of Islam had the center section.

The tables in the back and along the walls were separated by hoods. If you weren't from that hood, sitting there would surely get your head cut off, literally Scanning the room, Wisdom looked for familiar faces. Not spotting any he turned to ask Brinks a question but couldn't shake the feeling that someone was watching him.

"What's wrong?" Brinks asked in a low whisper.

"I get the feeling I'm being watched." Wisdom answered.

"Your name was ringing on the streets so a lot of guys are sizing you up. We got word a guy name Snake has been making some noise about what he is going to do to you when you hit the hill. Don't look, he's the guy over there in the Army fatigues and white T-shirt.

He's been watching us since we came in the door." said Brinks grabbing Wisdom arm so that he wouldn't make a scene.

"I aint scared or running from no nigga." Wisdom said through clenched teeth as his blood pressure began to rise.

"That's what I heard but we're not about to crash out; don't allow your emotions to cause you to act in a manner that will be detrimental to yourself or others. Wink's working on the line serving. Get behind me, when he hands you your tray, grab the knife taped to the bottom and wrap the string around your hand. Big Hands will cause a commotion distracting the guards to the other side of the chow hall. We have the advantage because Snake doesn't know we're on to him. He'll be watching us and won't notice Turk who will throw some hot grease in his face. Hit him in the neck and chest, walk out the door and pass the knife off to Man-Man. Rain will have a change of clothes for you, go back to your cell and make sure no blood is on you." Brinks instructed.

"What about his friends?" Wisdom asked.

"A lot of guys have friends until they see his ass getting gutted. If anyone bucks, there are enough of us on deck throughout to entertain them properly." Brinks assured him.

Accepting his tray, Wisdom removed the knife, wrapping the string around his hand. Following behind Brinks as Snake busied himself trying to see what the commotion was that Big Hands had start, he never noticed Turk sliding up the wall hot grease in hand.

"AHHHHHHHHIHHHHH" Turk tossed the hot grease in Snakes face, sliding back down the wall without being noticed, as Snake attempted to wipe the hot grease off, taking skin with it.

"You wanted to see me?" Wisdom growled in a menacing tone before plunging the knife into Snake's neck causing blood to splatter onto the walls.

Snake tried to fight back with little benefit. Swiftly pulling the knife out, leaving a hole the size of a golf ball, Wisdom rammed the steel rod into Snake's chest so hard sending it completely through his body cavity, hitting the brick wall Snake stood against.

"Look at me, I did this to you." Wisdom growled as he removed the knife before ramming it through Snake a second time.

"Come on, you're going to kill him." Wink said sliding up behind Wisdom tugging at his arm.

"I know." Wisdom spat trying to remove the knife, not quite finished with Snake.

"You've proved your point; now let's get out of here." Wink reasoned, while looking around for the guards and other threats.

As Wisdom tried to remove the knife, the suction from the second shot made the knife hard to pullout.

"Leave it, let's go!" Wink told Wisdom. Sliding down the wall, following the direction Turk went; Wisdom found Man-Man waiting and explained what had happened.

"Okay, grab the clothes from Rain and change quickly." Man-Man instructed while keeping an eye out for the guards.

Quickly taking off all his clothes, Wisdom gave them to Rain who immediately dropped them in a bucket of bleach.

"Go to your cell, they'll be around checking hands and looking for bloody cloths." Rain said picking up the bucket headed for the prison laundry.

After entering the cell, Wisdom hopped onto his bunk, falling back on his pillow

"I'm supposed to be trying to work my way out of prison. What a way to start things off" he said to himself before closing his eyes.

CHAPTER SIX

Lying back, Wisdom began to think about the day this nightmare began. After returning from the car show, spirits were high with Dammoe bring home the best custom classic car award.

They were turning off Hanley onto Martin Luther King entering Kinloch, as Dammoe rolled to a stop at the stop sign, police cars came from everywhere surrounding them.

"Turn off your engine and place your hands were we can see them!" came a loud voice over the bullhorn. Knowing that this could get ugly real quick, Wisdom was the first to comply. Officer's rushed over to the cars, pointing guns, screaming for them to exit the car slowly while keeping their hands in the air. Wisdom's crew was quickly cuffed without incident. Captain Smith exited his car making a beeline for Wisdom.

"Mr. Jones, we've been waiting on you to return. You see I knew that it was just a matter of time before I got something on you." said Captain Smith with a smirk on his face.

"I invoke my Fifth Amendment right to remain silent; I want my lawyer." Wisdom said calmly paying his words no attention.

"As you wish, Mr. Jones." said Captain Smith with a shit eating grin.

"Bring Mr. Jones with us, search the rest of them and their cars, and if you find ANYTHING charge them." Instructed Captain Smith

Wisdom was placed in the backseat of a police car. He wondered if this was Detective Brown's way of saying that he wanted more money but the thought quickly vanished when he realized he didn't see Detective Brown anywhere. So this was all Captain Smith's doing Wisdom thought to himself.

Wisdom was finger printed, photographed and placed into a cell, moments before Jason Rockford, followed by his assistant came bursting through the door looking for whoever was in charge.

"My name is Jason Rockford, Attorney at law, I represent Mr. Jones." Mr. Rockford told the Captain.

"Good because he's going to need a good lawyer." Stated Captain Smith leaning up against a file cabinet.

"What are the charges?" Mr. Rockford asked.

"Two counts murder in the first degree." said Captain Smith

"Based on what evidence?" Mr. Rockford questioned.

"You can talk to the prosecuting attorney about that Mr. Rockford. We are transporting Mr. Jones to St. Louis County within the hour." Said the Captain.

"I would like to speak with my client first." Mr. Rockford told Captain Smith.

"You have five minutes." Captain Smith told him. Mr. Rockford was led back to the cell Wisdom was being held in with a couple of drunks.

"Why did they arrest me?" asked Wisdom as soon as he saw Mr. Rockford.

"Murder." said Mr. Rockford

"What?" ask an astonished Wisdom

"You're being charged with two counts of first degree murder. The Caption said you will be transported to St. Louis County in a few minutes." said Mr. Rockford

"What will my bond be?" Wisdom ask

"I don't know, these are some serious charges that carry the death penalty, you may not get bond. If I can get you a bond, how much can you raise?" asked Mr. Rockford

"Whatever is needed!" stated Wisdom

"Okay I'm going to start my investigation now while everything's fresh. I'll stop by to see you in the morning."Mr. Rockford assured him.

"Ok, a retainer will be brought to you tomorrow." Wisdom replied.

"I've already been paid in full." Mr. Rockford informed Wisdom before walking off.

Wisdom was booked in the St. Louis County Jail and then placed in the Red Zone where the guys with the most serious cases were housed.

The Red Zone was made up of eight man cells with a toilet, sink, shower, phone and television. Wisdom was placed in A-2 with several guys that he knew from the streets.

"What's up Wisdom?" ask Big Black lighting up when he saw Wisdom walks through the gates.

"Nothing much Black, how long you been here?" Wisdom asked, surprised to see Big Black locked up.

"A couple of days." Answered Big Black

"And you aint posed bond? I know you aint broke?" said Wisdom

"Ha-ha, naw, they got a parole hold on me."

"For what?" ask Wisdom curious

"This chick I stopped fucking with told my PO that I went to the fight in Vegas."

"Damn." Said Wisdom

"What they got you for?" Big Black inquired changing the subject.

"Couple of bodies but I don't know who." Wisdom answered

"Damn, that's some serious shit" said Big Black

"It's all good, I'm going to beat it," said Wisdom confident in what he was saying.

"I hope so" said Big Black

"Don't worry, I'm good." stated Wisdom.

"O'yea, Trap and Gant are in here, they're on visit." Said Big Black before getting back to his book.

"Cool, I need to make a few calls." said Wisdom

After putting his things away Wisdom grabbed the phone and dialed Sky's number.

"Riiiiiiiiiiing. Riiiiiiiiiiing."

"Hello,"

"You have collect call from the St. Louis County Jail from Wisdom.
If you would like to accept the call press 5 if you would......."

"BEEP, "

"You may begin your conversation now" said the automated voice.

"Wisdom, what's going on, they say you've been charged with murder? asked an upset Sky

"I really don't know what they're talking about. My lawyer is doing his investigation and will be up to see me tomorrow. "Wisdom said

"I need you out here Wisdom." said Sky crying

"I'll be out once the dust settles. I need for you to stay focused on what you're doing, don't worry about me," Wisdom instructed her.

"I'm focused but I'm still worry about you." Sky countered

"You have the building and your business plan ready. Have you thought of a name for you modeling agency?" Wisdom asked.

"I haven't come up with anything I really like. I need to soon so I can get incorporated." Sky said

"What about Brick House Modeling Agency?" Wisdom suggested.

"I like that." said Sky smiling.

"Get it done then." said Wisdom

"I'm on it." she promised

"I need for you to look after Dank and Young Gunner while I'm gone. Make sure they stay in school and out of trouble." Wisdom requested

"Wisdom you know how they can be." said Sky

"Yea, but they respect you. Dank has three months before going off to college. Younger Gunner has one semester left. I don't want anything to get them off track." said Wisdom

"I'll do what I can but you need to talk to them so that we're all on the same page." Sky said knowing that it wouldn't be easy keeping things together without him being there.

"I will but if they give you any problems, let Uncle Ronnie know." said Wisdom

"Okay." said Sky

"I need to make a few more calls to try to get things straighten out." Wisdom told her

"Okay, call me back when you get a chance, we need to talk." said Sky

"I will." said Wisdom

As Wisdom was hanging up the phone Trap and Gant were coming through the gates.

"Wisdom what you doing locked up? said Trap giving him a pound

"It's all part of the game." said Wisdom

"I know your guys are coming to get you?" asked Gant giving him a pound also.

"No doubt if they set a bond." said Wisdom

"You on some RICO type shit?" asked Trap

"Naw, a couple of bodies that I know nothing about." replied Wisdom

"Damn, Wisdom. I know that high priced lawyer you be using will get you off." said Gant

"Yea, he's working his show as we speak. I need to make another call, I'll holler at yall when I get off." said Wisdom starting to feel uncomfortable talking about his case

Riiiiiiiiiiing, Riiiiiiiiiiing.

"Hello."

"You have collect call from the St. Louis County Jail from: Wisdom. If you would like to accept press 5 if you would..."

"BEEP,"

"You may begin your conversation now."

"Wisdom, what's up my nigga?" said young Gunner excited to talk to him.

"What I tell you about using that word?" Wisdom asked him in a clammy but firm tone.

"My bad." said Young Gunner.

"How's everyone doing?" Wisdom inquired.

"Man, they walking around like we just had your funeral."

"Before you pass the phone around, you and I need to have a talk. You graduate in a year and will be headed off to college." Wisdom said letting his words sink in.

"I don't ..." Young Gunner was saying before Wisdom cut him off.

"This isn't a democracy, you don't get a vote. You are going to college! Sky will make sure money continues to be placed in your college account. Anything that you want within reason will be given to you as long as you stay out of trouble and your grades are good. You understand me?" Wisdom asked him.

"Yes" said Young Gunner knowing that he couldn't win when it came to Wisdom.

"I was going to surprise you but now is a good time. I bought you a Yukon, I'll tell Sky to give you the keys." Said Wisdom.

"Oh, shit, you bought me a Yukon." yelled young Gunner jumping up and down.

"You deserve it, now let me speak to Dammoe." Wisdom said smiling. Wisdom could hear Young Gunner telling everyone.

"Wisdom bought me a Yukon!"

"Wisdom, what's the news asked Dammoe grabbing the phone.

"Don't know it's still early."

"I need for you to continue to follow the plan that was laid out. Stay focused, keep everyone out of trouble, and continue to move as a team. If people think we are divided or weak, they will try us. Wisdom instructed.

"I feel you bro, we got this out here, and you just handle that in there." Dammoe guaranteed him.

"I will, let me holler at Sleeper." Said Wisdom

"Wisdom, you know how we do, how can I help?" asked Sleeper grabbing the phone.

"Follow the script that we laid out. You and Dammoe have the ability to keep us on top." Wisdom said but knowing that it would be a challenge.

"Okay, but we gone get to the bottom of this." Said Sleeper.

"No doubt." Wisdom replied.

"Put Dank on the phone." Wisdom said

"Hello." Dank said accepting the phone.

"You're off to college in three months. I need you to stay focused on that."

"Wisdom, I ain't going anywhere if you're not here!" said Dank.

"I know how you are feeling but you will be hurting the family if you don't go. This is what we've worked so hard for." said Wisdom

"I know but it don't feel right without you here." said Dank.

"I'll be free soon but you need to stay focused. Sky will make sure you and Young Gunner are good."

"You know I got my own money." said Dank

"Yea, I know but Sky will make sure that everything is everything with you two because I want it this way." said Wisdom.

"Okay, if you need something, just holler Wisdom." said Dank.

"Thanks, Dank. Let me speak to Uncle Ronnie."

"Uncle Ronnie, Wisdom wants to speak to you" yelled Dank.

"Hello, Wisdom you know I don't like talking on these damn things." Uncle Ronnie said accepting the phone.

"Nice hearing your voice too Uncle Ronnie" Wisdom replied trying to lighten the situation.

"Are they treating you right in there?"

"I'm good. Listen, I really don't know what's going on. I need for you to keep an eye out for anything that looks out of place."

"Even with our people" asked Uncle Ronnie?"

"Everybody, something just doesn't feel right." replied Wisdom.

"No problem, I'm on it." said Uncle Ronnie pondering Wisdom's request.

"I'll send you a message once I hear something." Wisdom said before ending the call.

CHAPTER SEVEN

Sleep eluded Wisdom; he tossed and turned all night anticipating the visit from his lawyer. Although Wisdom covered his tracks at all times, something about Caption Smith's smirk made him feel uncomfortable. He knew when the police didn't ask questions, they already had the answers, and they didn't ask any.

"Wisdom Jones you have a legal visit." Office Star yelled through the bars.

Hopping off the bunk, Wisdom quickly made his way to the visiting room. Mr. Rockford was waiting alone when Wisdom entered the attorney visiting room.

"You look like shit." Wisdom said looking at his crumpled attire.

"I've been up all night trying to piece this together."Mr. Rockford admitted.

"Thanks"

"Wisdom you are being charged with the murders of Mike Gray and Larry Gray. They were murder in Kinloch Park on July 12, 2006 between 9:45 and 10:15 pm." said Mr. Rockford. Before I go any further, you know how I work Wisdom. I don't care about the victim or any rap partner. All I care about is you. Here's a copy of the police report, it's rather thin. There's no physical evidence linking anyone to the murders but they have an eyewitness whom they are keeping secret." Mr. Rockford said handing Wisdom the police report.

"They have a witness saying they saw me commit the murders?" ask Wisdom shocked.

"Yes, the witness is saying that there were three masked men but he recognized you because of your eyes." said Mr. Rockford.

"Man that's some bullshit, I ain't did nothing." Wisdom screamed.

"Calm down Wisdom, that's a very weak identification. We need to find out who the witness is." said Mr. Rockford who needed Wisdom to focus so that they could win.

"Can they do that?" asked Wisdom

"Yes, in cases dealing with children to protect them."said Mr. Rockford

"So you think their eyewitness is a minor?" asked Wisdom.

"Let's not jump to conclusions; something just isn't right about this. First, these murders happened last year. If they had an eyewitness why would they wait so long to come after you? with a weak identification and no physical evidence, there's something more motivating this prosecution." said Mr. Rockford.

"Like what?" asked Wisdom.

"Election time, there are a lot of tough on crime ads running on television. With the passing of the 85% and Clinton giving states all that money to build prisons. Politicians need to make some examples to let the people see their taxes dollars are hard at work keeping them safe." said Mr. Rockford

"Whoa, I'm no Pablo Escobar or John Gotti?" Wisdom said in his defense.

"Doesn't matter, you've caught someone's attention who plans on using you as a pawn to advance their career." said Mr. Rockford.

"So what do we do?" asked Wisdom.

"First we find out who the players are. Once we find out who's behind this, then we can better understand how to fight it. Most importantly, we need to find out who the eyewitness is so that we can prepare." said Mr. Rockford.

"And if we don't find out who the witness is before trial?" asked Wisdom.

"The case is still weak Wisdom, but we will have to prepare on the fly." said Mr. Rockford

"I don't like the sound of that. Should I get another lawyer?" asked Wisdom.

"Wisdom, a good lawyer won't tell you things just to make you feel better or stroke your ego. We must deal with the reality of this situation. I don't have to tell you how hard I fight, you already know from experience. If you feel that I'm not the man for the job, I'll return your money and respect your decision." said Mr. Rockford sitting back in his chair.

"Naw, you're the best, I'm riding with you." said Wisdom after giving it some thought.

"Wise decision! Look over the copy of your police report, memorize it and let me know of any inconsistencies you notice. I waived your preliminary hearing; they were going to bound you over anyway for trial. Bond was set at two million dollars cash only." said Mr. Rockford.

"Two million dollars, that's a ransom." Wisdom remarked

"Yea, we won't try to make it, it wouldn't be wise. I will go talk to the judge about them not disclosing the identity of the eyewitness and file a motion for a fast and speedy trial." Mr. Rockford explained.

"Yea, we need to get things moving." Wisdom said not liking the direction things were going.

"Wisdom, remember if this is what I expect, then don't look for any favorable rulings from the judge." Mr. Rockford warned before standing to leave.

All eyes were on Wisdom as he entered the cell. Everyone basically knew that attorney visit went really well or really bad. From the look on Wisdom's face, things were not going according to his plan.

Sitting on his bunk, Wisdom began to formulate a plan. He knew that in order to survive, he had to fight and to fight he had to be in shape mentally, physically and spiritually He would keep to himself, avoided trouble, miserable or unlucky people while making a conscience effort to read at least one book a week outside of law ranging from the economy, business, to history so that his mind would stay sharp.

He would become a quiet man caged like a wild animal who guards and inmates alike would watch, and probably think that he would lose his mind reading all the time but in truth he knew that if he succumb to jail life then and only then would he loose his mind and freedom forever.

With long terms goals intact: (a) Strengthen his faith in God (b) changing the way he thought and (c) finding out who was behind all this, Wisdom was on a mission.

CHAPTER EIGHT

Dammoe and Kim's serious lovemaking, heavy breathing, slow kisses, and lots of licking lasted until both reached their climax. The sweet smell of hot, sticky, wet pussy consumed Dammoe as he parted Kim's mouth with his lips. Moving downward, he pushes her breasts together, sucks and kisses her nipples, while inserting his fingers into her.

"Oh God ... too much, please, Dammoe, I can't take this," she yelled in ecstasy, while he fingered her clit, rubbing her juices throughout and wiggling his fingers in and out of her vigorously.

"That's right, baby, come hard for me," he said as he kissed her passionately.

Multiple orgasms took control of her and all she could do was give into the pleasure.

"Dammoe, baby, uuuuuuuuuuuuuh ... aaaahhh! Shit, this is so good! "

Knowing that Dammoe would be tearing up her pussy for another three hours if she let him; Kim forced him onto his back and began to suck his dick deciding to swallowing all that he had would be quicker. Just as she finished, his phone began to ring.

Riiiiiiiiling, Riiiiiiiiing.

"Hello"

"You have collect call from the St. Louis County Jail from: Wisdom."

"If you would like to accept press 5 if you would...

"You may begin your conversation now."

Wisdom, what did the lawyer say?" ask Dammoe still trying to catch his breath.

"It's still early, he doesn't know much." Wisdom answered.

"Shit, with all the money we paying him, he better get you out soon." Dammoe said.

"Calm down, these things take time. How are things on your end?" asked Wisdom.

"Things are going well, you have nothing to worry about." said Dammoe.

"Stay focused and don't get caught up on the fruits of the hustle." Wisdom warned.

"We got this bro." said Dammoe.

"I need you to find Uncle Ronnie. Tell him I said don't forget to meet with the real estate agent at 3:00 today." said Wisdom.

"You buying a house?" asked Dammoe

"Investing in the future." Wisdom replied before ending the call.

After hanging up, he made his way back to his bunk to begin strategizing.

"Looks like you got a lot on your mind. Is everything alright?" asked Big Black

"Yea, I'm good, just got some things to think about." said Wisdom.

"Sounds more like you have some strategizing to do. Here read this, it will give you some ideas." said Big Black.

"Book of Five Rings, how is this going to help?" asked Wisdom

"It will help in shaping your thoughts. You're smart no doubt Wisdom; however you lack formal training which will compliment your street knowledge. Big Black pointed out

"Huh?" ask Wisdom

"Most people get caught because they haven't planned things all the way through. Take yourself for example; you wouldn't be sitting here if you had the right connections. That lawyer you got is good but he doesn't control anything or make the rules." said Big Black

"If you know all of this then why are you here?" said Wisdom

"Read the book." answered Big Black getting back to the one he was reading.

"What are you reading?" ask wisdom

"Why Should White Men Have All the Fun by Reginald F. Lewis." answered Big Black

"What is it about?" ask Wisdom

"A smart black man who beat the white man at his own game in business." answered Big Black

"You getting out the game?" ask Wisdom

"I've never been in the game." stated Big Black

"Nigga you think I'm a rat or something?" Wisdom said getting to his feet.

"You need to calm down. A game is something you play. Look around you, do you think these people are playing?" asked a serious Big Black getting back to his book.

Sitting down Wisdom began to read the book and his eyes were open to strategies he'd used unknowingly as well as some that had been used on him. Wisdom was so wrapped up in the book; he didn't realize how much time had passed.

"Wisdom Jones, you have a visit." yelled Guard Walker. Exiting the cell his mind was still on the things that he'd spent the afternoon learning. Entering the visiting booth he couldn't believe his eyes.

"Damn, Uncle Ronnie, didn't know you had it in you. You look like you just stepped off the cover of GQ." said Wisdom admiring the tailored suit that he wore.

"Sleep on me, get your head lumped youngin. Said Uncle Ronnie smiling.

"I won't."

"I went to see your lawyer; he gave me a copy of the police report. This is some bullshit, unless the witness is a child they have no right to withhold their identity according to your lawyer" said Uncle Ronnie frustrated.

"Yea, I've been doing some research myself and he's right. I just don't think that witness is a child." said Wisdom

"It's not impossible." countered Uncle Ronnie reaching into his pocket, Wisdom pulled out the letter he'd written earlier and held it up to the glass.

Uncle Ronnie,
It's not a child, they would've been brought charges sooner. This
seems like someone got caught up and gave me up to save
themselves. Been giving that a lot thought but I'm coming up
empty. It wasn't our family because if it was they would have
given the police more damaging evidence.
Think about it, they didn't kick in any of our spots looking for
evidence. It appears that Caption Smith is leading this
investigation, keeping Det. Brown out of the loop. I want you to
follow Caption Smith and see where it leads.

Wisdom took the letter, ripped it into tiny pieces and ate it. Uncle Ronnie stood nodded and walked off, a man on a mission.

CHAPTER NINE

Wisdom's relationship with Sky had become tense since she moved to Atlanta after seeing Dank off to college. Her modeling agency had taken off keeping her busy; however she always found the time to write and make sure that his books were right.

Young Gunner refused to leave with her and only after being assured by Uncle Ronnie that he would attend college in the fall did she feel comfortable leaving him.

The judge denied Wisdom's motion for a fast and speedy trial so he'd been in the County Jail thirteen months. Most of his time was spent studying law and educating himself. Wisdom knew that he had to change his ways before they caught up with him. He vowed to become a businessman who gave and not took from the community when he was released.

Conversations with Dammoe and Sleeper were becoming rarer. The last he heard Dammoe had bought a 600 Benz and Sleeper a Hummer. He knew that it was only a matter of time before they found themselves in a cage, next to him. He couldn't help but notice how much things had change in such a short period of time.

"You ready to get this workout in?" asked Gant bringing Wisdom back to the present.

"No doubt, whatcha got in mind?" asks Wisdom

"Let's start with push-ups. Stand and face me. We'll do 10 sets of 10, then 10 sets of 9 until we reach 1." said Gant

"So we do 10, then stand up at the same time then go back down?" ask Wisdom

"Yep, ready youngin?" ask Gant

"Waiting on you." Wisdom replied

Wisdom was able to match Gant set for set the first 20 set. When they enter sets of 8, his lack of endurance started to show.

"Don't tell me you tired youngin?" ask Gant with a knowing smile.

"Doesn't matter, let's go." Wisdom replied getting down for the first set of 8

"Ronald Stone bunk and junk." screamed one of the Officers. Big Black was in the middle of a conversation with Trap when he heard his name being called.

"My train just pulled in." said Big Black giving Trap a pound.

"That's what it is; I'll see you when I get there. Said Trap

"Gant as long as I'm eating you eating dirty, take this number." said Big Black handing him a piece of paper.

"Wisdom, the knowledge you have acquired will help you with the battles you will encounter. Remember, Wisdom is the right use or exercise of knowledge and understanding. Thus Wisdom is in act, effect, or practice. If wisdom is to be considered as a faculty of the mind, it is the faculty of discerning or judging what is most just, proper and useful, and if it is to be considered as an acquirement, it is the knowledge and use of what is best, most just, most proper, most conducive to prosperity or happiness. Wisdom in the first sense, or practical wisdom, is nearly synonymous with discretion. It differs somewhat from prudence, in this respect; prudence is the exercise of sound judgment in avoiding evils; wisdom is the exercise of sound judgment either in avoiding evils or attempting good. Prudence then is a species, of which wisdom is the genus." said Big Black winking at Wisdom

"Thanks Big Black, you dropped a lot of knowledge on me. Take it easy out there, I'll see you soon." said Wisdom.

"Wisdom, man is most unique when he turns an obstacle into an opportunity." said Big Black exiting the cell.

"He's about to ball out of control. Wisdom, you start trial tomorrow. How you feeling?" ask Gant who pled guilty to 15 years Fed time last week.

"I'm good, just ready to get this over with." Wisdom replied not sure how this was going to turn out.

"I wish you the best man but just remember no matter what happens. If you stop thinking, you start stinking." said Gant giving him a serious look.

"No doubt." said Wisdom.

"Let's finish this workout. You've had enough time to rest." said Gant smiling.

****

Wisdom was a changed man, not only physically because of his daily workout routine he maintained. His thought had been elevated allowing him to see things clearer.

Awaking early Monday morning, shaved and showered, before reading the Bible and praying.

After breakfast he was led over to the courthouse to begin the fight of his life. Entering the holding cage, Mr. Rockford appeared soon after handing him one black and one blue tailored Armani suit that Sky had brought for him.

"I still don't know who the witness is." Mr. Rockford admitted to Wisdom.

"We'll deal with it the best we can." Wisdom replied changing into the black suit.

"I don't like this shit." Mr. Rockford said before walking off.

After getting dressed, Wisdom looked at himself in the mirror. What he saw only reassured him that this was how he should look and dress once free.

Upon entering the courtroom, Wisdom spotted Sky sitting in the front with Uncle Ronnie, Dammoe, and Sleeper sitting behind her.

The prosecutor, Tom "Hang em' High" Green, strolled into the courtroom, followed closely by two assistant prosecutors and a paralegal, he is up for Re-election, we would surely make a circus out of this Wisdom thought to himself, knowing the Prosecutor Green didn't try many cases but when he did, he always put on a award winning show.

"Everyone please stand, the Honorable Walter Reed." The bailiff shouted getting everyone's attention, as Judge Reed exited his chambers quickly making his way onto the bench.

"You all may be seated. We are here in the matter of the State of Missouri v. Wisdom Jones.

Mr. Rockford, Mr. Green are you gentleman ready to proceed?" ask Judge Reed

"Yes, your honor." Mr. Green replied standing to show his respect for the court.

"Your Honor there's still the matter of the identity of the only eyewitness or evidence linking my client to these murders that hasn't been disclosed." said Mr. Rockford standing as well.

"Your Honor, if I may?" asked Mr. Green

"You may Mr. Green." said Judge Reed looking over his glasses.

"Your Honor, Mr. Jones and his bandit of killers…."

"Your Honor there is no such evidence." Mr. Rockford quickly injected while shooting Mr. Green a mean mug.

"Mr. Rockford, the jury's not present, save your objection." said Judge Reed waving him off.

"As I was saying your Honor, Mr. Jones and his associates have a reputation for being high level drug traffickers who kill for sport. The state didn't want to put our only witness life in jeopardy." argued Mr. Green

"Your Honor, the defense has the right to know if the witness got a deal or what other impeaching evidence may exist concerning him. Without his identify my client's right to Due Process will be denied." Rockford countered.

"The defense will be given 15 minutes to speak with the witness before he takes the stand. Any impeaching evidence including any deals or criminal record will be provided to the defense at that time." said Judge Reed.

"Your honor there is no legal precedent for such a ruling. The state hasn't alleged that the witness is a child." Stated an angry Mr. Rockford

"Mr. Rockford, I've made my ruling. If you don't like it, take it up on appeal." yelled an agitated Judge Reed

"Appeal, Appeal!!!," shouted Sleeper getting to his feet.

"Order, Order, bailiff remove that man from the courtroom." ordered Judge Reed. Sleeper was removed from the courtroom and jury selection began shortly thereafter. After numerous questions and objections nine men and three women were sworn in to decide Wisdom's fate.

Leaving the courtroom, Mr. Green quickly returned limping on an AK-47. Once in front of the jury, he turned facing them and: BOOM, BOOM, BOOM, BOOH, BOOH, BOOM, BOOM, BOOM, BOOM,BOOM, BOOM, BOOM, BOOM, BOOM, BOOM, BOOM, BOOM, BOOM, BOOM, BOOM, opening fire using blanks, scaring the shit out of everyone, Mr. Green emptied the clip.

"This is what Wisdom Jones did to these two poor men" Mr. Green said with a disgusted look on his face pointing at Wisdom.

"Objection, Objection your honor. We want a mistrial, Mr. Green has lost his damn mind." yelled Mr. Rockford jumping out of his seat.

"Overruled, the jury is to disregard Mr. Green's actions and be guided by the evidence." Judge Reed calmly said.

Mr. Green's opening statement was short describing Bam and Jinks as being victims of a senseless murder. He told the jury that they weren't pillars of the community but didn't deserve to be mowed down by Wisdom and his murderous crew.

Mr. Rockford rose, and explained to the jury that this was a case of rush to judgment and the state had the wrong man, and that the state didn't have one shred of creditable evidence, instead will resort to outrageous tactics to scare them into convicting his innocent client.

Dr. Gordon, medical examiner, who performed the autopsies on the bodies, was the first to take the stand. Mr. Green spent several hours going over the gruesome details of the wounds sustained by the victims before turning the witness over to the defense.

"Mr. Rockford, would you like to cross examination Dr. Gordon?" Judge Reed inquired.

"No your honor." stated Mr. Rockford scribbling down notes.

"What are you doing?" asked an angry Wisdom

"Wisdom let me do my job. He testified to what we all already know; that they're dead. There is nothing that I could ask to change that." said Mr. Rockford setting down his pen, looking wisdom in the eyes.

Detective Brown was next to take the stand. With little information to provide, Detective Brown told the jury that when he arrived Bam and Jinks were already dead and there were no eyewitness.

Captain Smith, followed, testifying that when he arrived at the scene Detective Brown reported to him what he told the jury. Then he dropped a bombshell, telling the jury that a little over a year after the murders, he received information from a confidential informant who had witnessed the murders.

Question: Captain Smith, without revealing the informants name, please tell the jury what he told you. (Mr. Green)

Answer: I was approached by the informant; he felt his life was in danger because he had witnessed the murders in Kinloch Park.

Question: Did he say why? (Mr. Green)

Answer: He said that Sleeper, one of Mr. Jones associates approached him one night, telling him he knew he had witness the murders and that he better keep his mouth shut or he would kill his family.

Objection: Hearsay (Mr. Rockford), jumping to his feet.

Overruled: You may continue (Judge Reed)

Question: Captain Reed, what did the witness say he witnessed. (Mr. Green)

Answer: He stated that he was in Kinloch Park when he saw three masked gunmen open fire on the victim's.

Question: Did the witness ask you for a deal or any special treatment. (Mr. Green)

Answer: No

"No further questions." said Mr. Green taking his seat.

"Mr. Rockford, your witness." said Judge Reed

"Thank you Your Honor." Mr. Rockford said standing

Question: Captain Smith is it normal for Police Captions to lead murder investigations? (Mr. Rockford)

Answer: What do you mean by normal?

Question: Is it a part of your normal job duties? (Mr. Rockford)

Answer: Normal, no. However, being that the information was brought directly to me and I wanted to protect the witness, so I decide to handle it myself.

Question: Do you own a condo and boat at the Lake of the Ozarks? (Mr. Rockford)

Objection, relevancy (Mr. Green)

"Your Honor, the City of Kinloch has had several public officials imprisoned for taking bribes or robbing drug dealers. Given Captain Smith's yearly income of $60,000, it's hard to imagine how he can afford a half a million dollar Condo or a $350,000 boat!

"That has no relevancy in this trial." said Judge Reed.

I have no further question." said Mr. Rockford taking his seat having planted the seed for the jury.

"You may step down Captain Smith. We will take a 30 minute recess. At that time the defense will be permitted to speak with the witness for the time allotted and give any impeachment evidence." said Judge Reed

"We're getting our ass handed to us." Wisdom said leaning over whispering into Mr. Rockford's ear.

"I told you it was political, now you see for yourself. I'll be right back; I need to go interview this witness." Mr. Rockford said before getting to his feet.

Mr. Rockford left Wisdom sitting there thinking about who the witness could possibly be, it could only one person: Dirty D, he concluded.

Mr. Rockford entered the holding room interrupting the conversation the Mr. Green was having with his witness.

"This is Mr. Jones lawyer, Mr. Rockford. Answer the question that he has for you truthfully." Mr. Green said hoping that Mr. Rockford hadn't heard any of their conversation.

"What is your name?" asked Mr. Rockford

"Todd Davis." the witness answered.

"Have you been given a deal or promised anything by anyone?" asked Mr. Rockford.

"No" answered Todd.

"Do you have any prior convictions?" asked Mr. Rockford.

"No" answered Todd.

"Why did it take you so long to come forward?" ask Mr. Rockford.

"I wasn't going to come forward until Sleeper threatened me." Todd answered

"What do you think you saw?" asked Mr. Rockford.

"I saw Wisdom shoot Bam and Jinks." Todd said firmly.

"How do you know it was Wisdom?" ask Mr. Rockford.

"I've been knowing him my whole life, I would know him anywhere, even with a mask on." answered Todd

"Thank you Mr. Davis. Is he telling the truth about a deal or prior record?" Mr. Rockford asked Mr. Green.

"Yes" Mr. Green answered too quickly. Mr. Rockford left the room shaken, he knew that Todd Davis had been coached but didn't know how he could get the jury to see it. Entering the courtroom, he went straight to the defense table to speak with Wisdom.

"Do you know Todd Davis?" Mr. Rockford asked Wisdom leaning over so that only he could hear him.

"Name doesn't ring a bell." Wisdom replied

"He says he's known you his entire life." said Mr. Rockford.

"Is he really black, 5'9, 165 lbs., with braids?" asked Wisdom.

"No" answered Mr. Rockford.
Wisdom was now dumb founded not knowing who it could possibly be. As his mind continued to race, the bailiff entered the court.

"All rise the court is now back in session, the Honorable Judge Reed presiding"

"You may be seated, bring in the jury." Judge Reed said taking the bench.

"Mr. Green, call your next witness." said Judge Reed.

"The state calls Todd Davis." Mr. Green said standing. To everyone's amazement, Rex entered the courtroom, taking the stand without looking in

Wisdom's direction. Wisdom couldn't believe his eyes; never would he have imagined that Rex would do such a thing.

Please state your name for the record? asked (Mr. Green)

Answer: Todd Davis.

Question: Where do you live? (Mr. Green)

Answer: Kinloch, in St. Louis County.

Question: Do you know Wisdom Jones?

Answer: Yes.

Question: How do you know him?

Answer: His mother and my mother are sisters

A pin drop could be heard in the courtroom from this revelation. Mr. Rockford looked at Wisdom out of the corner of his eye in disbelief.

Question: Where you present in Kinloch Park on the night of July 12, 2006?

Answer: Yes

Question: What were you doing?

Answer: Talking to Dirty D.

Question: Then what happened?

Answer: Bam called Dirty D over to the bench to talk. They talk for a minute then I saw Dirty D break out running and that's when I heard the gunshots.

Question: Who did you see commit these murders?

Answer: Wisdom Jones (Rex pointed at Wisdom)

(Mr. Green): Please let the record reflect that the witness has identified Mr. Jones and pointed him out at the defense table).

Question: Mr. Davis, if the shooters had on masks. How do you know it was Wisdom?

Answer: I recognized the build of his body and saw his eyes.

Question: Have you received a deal or any favorable treatment in exchange for your testimony?

Answer: No.

Question: Why didn't you come forward sooner?

Answer: Because family protects family.

Question: So why did you come forward?

Answer: Because one of Wisdom's goons threatened to kill me and my family if I ever talked. I didn't have any intentions on talking but when I saw that Wisdom would kill his own family to keep his secret; I felt I had to tell.

No further question. (Mr. Green)

"Mr. Rockford, it's your turn." said Judge Reed

"One second Judge." Mr. Rockford said before leaning over to confer with Wisdom.

"His mother and your mother are sisters?" Mr. Rockford asked totally confused.

"Fuck naw, that nigga ain't no kin to me." Wisdom spat.

"So you telling me he made that up?" ask Mr. Rockford Wisdom making sure that he was clear.

"No doubt, look the deck is stacked; just do the best you can." Wisdom replied before sitting back in his seat thinking that it was him Rex should be scared of, the man who would soon snatch his soul, instead of the prosecutor who could do nothing but inconvenience him.

"I'm ready Judge." Mr. Rockford said getting to his feet.

"Judge may we have a recess?" asked Mr. Green catching Mr. Rockford by surprise.

"We will take a ten minute recess." said Judge Reed

"John, may I speak with you outside?" asked Mr. Green, leaning over the table.

"Yea, sure, what's up?" asked Mr. Rockford following him out into the hallway.

"His testimony was too powerful for you to impeach John. I'll offer your guy murder two: four life sentences with parole ran into one, he'll be out in 25 1/2. He has 5 minutes to think about it," said Mr. Green

"He won't take it." Mr. Rockford replied

"As his lawyer, you must present the deal to him." Mr. Green said.

"I will." said Mr. Rockford retuning to the courtroom ready for a confrontation that he didn't want to have with Wisdom.

Mr. Rockford leaned over and whispered into Wisdom's ear,

"I'm obligated to tell you this. Mr. Green has offered you life with parole; you'll be out in 25 1/2." said Mr. Rockford

"You in on it too?" asked Wisdom

"Show me some respect Wisdom. I've fought for you and kept you out of prison for years. I'm not saying I think you are guilty but with the life you live getting fucked around is all a part of the game." Mr. Rockford countered who was mad at Wisdom for getting himself in such a situation.

"What?" said a visibly upset Wisdom.

"Do you remember what I told you the last time that I got you off that "undisciplined violence" with be harshly dealt with, do you remember that?" ask Mr. Rockford who was upset himself because he truly liked Wisdom.

"What does that have to do with anything?" ask Wisdom

"It has to do with everything, Wisdom. They commit murder but it's how they do it. When you have someone shooting an AK-47 in the middle of Kings Highway, it scares the shit out of people. Wisdom, this isn't Iraq. They feel that an example has to be made or it will continue to happen. I know that your situation isn't exactly what I just described but you get my point." said Mr. Rockford

"I ain't snatching life with parole; fuck him. Let's get this show on the road." said Wisdom looking Mr. Rockford in the eyes.

Walking back into the hallway, feeling a bit defeated Mr. Rockford, gave Mr. Green the thumbs down. Not knowing how to counter such damaging evidence, Mr. Rockford was truly lost.

Mr. Green reentered the courtroom, walked up to the defense table and stopped. Looking Wisdom in the eye, he grabbed his tie and held the bottom of it up in the air like a man hanging from a tree and then turned his head to the side like it was broken, before walking off.

"Anybody can get it, Wisdom, thought to himself as his blood boiled from the blatant act of disrespect.

Court resumed and after 30 minutes of trying to discredit Rex, Mr. Rockford took his seat.

"Mr. Rockford, will you call any witnesses?" asked Judge.

"No, your honor, the defense rest." said Mr. Rockford.

"Hold up!" said Wisdom grabbing his arm.

"Mr. Rockford, maybe you should consult with your client." said Judge Reed.

Mr. Rockford turned facing Wisdom,

"Wisdom, we are better off not trying to call any alibi witnesses. If the jury doesn't believe your alibi, you are defiantly going to prison. We don't have to prove where you where, all we have to prove is that you weren't at the scene of the murders." said Mr. Rockford.

"Ok" said Wisdom calming down a bit.

"The defense rests." said Mr. Rockford. Closing arguments began with Mr. Green recapping the testimony of Rex and pointing out the he had no reason to lie on his family. Mr. Rockford countered, pointing out all the inconsistencies in Rex's testimony. The judge read the jury instruction and gave the case to the jury for deliberation.

After one hour and forty five minutes of deliberation, Wisdom was found guilty.

CHAPTER TEN

"Rack 209." yelled an unfamiliar voice snapping out of his thoughts, Wisdom jumped off the bunk preparing himself for whatever.

"Good evening Wisdom, I'm Jamaal." Jamaal said stepping into the cell, closing the bars behind him. Sensing that this could quickly get out of control, Jamaal called out to Man-Man.

"Man-Man" Jamaal yelled

"Yea, what's up Jamaal?" answered Man-Man

"Just letting you know I'm off work." said Jamaal watching Wisdom.

Wisdom seeing that Jamaal was who he said he was jumped back onto his bunk, giving Jamaal the room he needed to get himself together.

"Wisdom, what happened today wasn't us flexing our muscles, we don't do that. Snakes' fatal mistake was his mouth; the tongue is a beast that most people can't control. Had he been smart he would have kept his thoughts to himself, while rocking you to sleep until he could crush you completely." said Jamaal as he washed his face and hands.

This dudes on some Art of War shit, Wisdom thought but didn't say anything.

"At times in this cage we must reach understanding with men but that's only when all other methods have been exhausted. Some guys thrive off violence but to fight and conquer in all your battles is not supreme excellence; supreme excellence consists in breaking the enemy's resistance without fighting. Sun Tzu." Jamaal continued.

"I'm feeling that, how did you know about today? Wisdom inquired.

"We've been planning it since we heard you were coming here. Somehow Snake found out you were coming and started running his mouth which set the wheels in motion." Answered Jamaal as he dried his hands.

"You have a nice collection of books. Your conversation reveals that you have spent your time wisely." Wisdom complimented him.

"Thank you, you should do the same thing Wisdom, when opportunities materialize they appear in different forms and from different directions then you expect. That is one of the tricks to opportunity. It has a sly habit of slipping in by the back door; often it comes disguised in the form of misfortune or temporary defeat. Perhaps this is why so many fail to recognize an opportunity. Yes, you are in prison but it's an opportunity none the less. Feel free to read any of the books on the shelf. I would recommend starting with As a Man Thinketh." said Jamaal handing him the book.

Wisdom sat with his back against the wall and began to read:

"The mind is the master power that molds and makes, and man is mind, and evermore he takes the tool of thought, and, shaping what he wills, brings forth a thousand joys, a thousand ills. He thinks in secret, and it comes to pass. "

Thought and Character

The saying, "as a man think" in his heart so he is, not only embraces the whole of a man's being, but is so comprehensive as to reach out to every condition and circumstance of his life. A man is literally what he thinks, his character being the complete sum of all his thoughts.

As the plant springs from, and could not be without, the seed, so every act of a man springs from the hidden seeds of thought, and could not have appeared without them. This applies equally to those acts called "spontaneous" and "unpremeditated" as to those, which are deliberately executed.

Act is the blossom of thought, joy and suffering is its fruits; thus does a man acquire in the sweet and bitter fruitage of his own cultivating thoughts.

"This is some real stuff, I like it," said Wisdom

"Thought you would enjoy it," Jamaal replied as he continued grooming himself before wiping the floor down, and then switching on the television clicking past BET, which caught wisdom's attention.

"You don't watch BET?" asked Wisdom setting the book down.

"I enjoy BET just as much as the next man, however men must understand that BET is Black ENTERTAINMENT Television. It is our duty to follow the local and national news. Then if time permits for entertainment, enjoy yourself." Jamaal answered

"Why watch the news?" ask Wisdom

"It keeps you abreast on things evolving in the world whether it's crime, news/ laws, politics, or health." Jamaal educated Wisdom

"What does that have to do with a guy serving life without the possibility of probation or parole?" asked Wisdom

"Let me tell you a story. There was this old white guy who lived on two walk, locked up for killing his wife. We called him Banker Bob because he owned a bank. Often when in the library researching issues on my case Banker Bob would walk by and nod, heading for the newspaper section. He did this for about four months, then one day stopped at the table. He asked me why I was wasting my time researching the law. I said I was trying out of prison. He laughed and said good connections and being prepared for an opportunity would take me further than any law books and then he walked off."

"He sounds like a nut basket." Wisdom said

"Far from it, when the governor died in a plane crash about a year later. During a news conference the Lieutenant Governor said he didn't have any political ambitions. Banker Bob used his connections to get a large bag of money to the Lieutenant Governor who gave him a full pardon before leaving office." said Jamaal

"Damn, he was thinking outside the box." said Wisdom impressed as his wheels began to spin.

"Not really, money is a gun, knowing when to pull the trigger is politics. He knew politics and how to make his money work for him but nothing else." said Jamaal

"Why would you need to know anything else when you have that?" ask Wisdom

"Man should strive to gain knowledge that covers a diverse range of things. Banker Bob was as smart as they come in the realm of finance and politics but nothing else." said Jamaal

"He was smart enough to get out of this cage." Argued Wisdom

"Yea, but he's that guy you passed on your way to that poker game. The damn fool murdered his second wife and threw the gun with his finger prints on it in the lake behind their house." said Jamaal dropping a bombshell on Wisdom.

Falling back onto his bunk, Wisdom couldn't believe his ears. No man who has lived in one of these cages for any amount of time could be that stupid, he thought to himself. His thoughts were interrupted by the opening of the cell bars for recreation release. Uncertain from the events that occurred earlier in the day, he didn't move. His street instincts told him that there would be retaliation, Jamaal was reading his thought.

"This is for showers. There won't be any recreation because of what happened earlier." Jamaal told him.

"Oh" Wisdom said not sure what else to say.

"You good, no one would make it off this walk alive if they came up here, believe that." Jamaal said before heading out the door to go take a shower.

Wisdom jumped off the bunk, grabbed is things, headed for the shower.

CHAPTER ELEVEN

On the streets Dammoe and Sleeper were partying like rock starts and blowing money fast, receiving the attention and credibility they always craved; however the business was suffering.

They decided to shut down the trap houses and focus only on moving weight, this strategy allowed them the time to jet set with rappers and models.

Wisdom had been behind The Walls for three years working in the prison's law library. Although Mr. Rockford hired the best appellate specialist and investigator to work on his appeal, wisdom's direct appeal and motion for post-conviction relief were denied.

The court claimed that there were errors throughout his trial but they were harmless. How an error could possibly be harmless when a man is serving life without parole was something that wisdom never understood.

Feeling that no one loves him like he loved himself, Wisdom decided to learn as much about the law as he possible could to ensure nothing was overlooked. Preoccupied, Wisdom hadn't reached out to Dammoe or Sleeper in quite some time but after hearing how they were moving, he knew that he had too.

"Riiiiiiiiing, Riiiiiiiiiiing"

"Hello"

"You have collect call from the Jefferson City Correctional Center from: Wisdom. If you would like to accept press 1 if you would to block this call press 7 "BEEP"

"You may begin your conversation now."

"Wisdom what's good?" asked Dammoe.

Wisdom ignored the question. "You allowed the recording to play all the way through. Were you debating on accepting the call?" Wisdom questioned.

"Naw, it wasn't nothing like that bro, you just caught me in the middle of something, you know what I mean?" said Dammoe.

"From what I hear, both of you are out there acting like donkey's" said Wisdom,

"Bro don't believe everything you hear in there." said Dammoe trying to reassure Wisdom that everything was fine.

"So it's not true that you just bought the new Aston Martin DB9 Lexani Custom Edition?" asked Wisdom

How the fuck did this nigga know this, I haven't even hit the streets in it yet? thought Dammoe.

"You wondering how I know? Dammoe I may be on the bench but I'm still in the game keeping score." Wisdom informed him.

"Wisdom we just blowing off a little steam, enjoying life, besides we're making sure your lawyers are paid and everyone is eating." Dammoe explained.

"The money that you're giving the lawyers and everyone else is scraps! I do numbers well." Wisdom reminded him.

"Wisdom, you don't understand. We aren't in the streets like that anymore. This way is better." said Dammoe

"You telling me that you aren't drawing attention with flashy cars, jewelry, front row seats at fights and being courtside with rappers at basketball games?" asked Wisdom

"We got this out here, just keep fighting in there. You will be good when you get home." said Dammoe

"I got to get off this phone, tell Sleeper that I'll catch up with him later," said Wisdom hanging up the phone disappointed in them.

Walking away from the phone, Wisdom couldn't believe how reckless Dammoe and Sleeper had become. It was as if all of the lessons that they'd learned had been forgotten. Hearing someone yell his name, Wisdom stopped, it was Rain.

"How are you doing?" Wisdom asked always happy to see Rain.

"To blessed to be depressed. Step in my cell and have a seat. What's bothering you?" Rain asked.

"My friends, whom I was raised up with like brothers have become donkeys and aren't playing by the rules." said Wisdom

"It's out of sight out of mind. Don't take that personal but when it's your time to leave this cage, you will remember some and reach back to them but life out there will take its toll. This is not to say that what they are doing is right at all." Rain explained

"Rain, they out there buying SLR Benzs and flossing drawing all type of attention to themselves." said Wisdom

"Wisdom, you did the same thing." said Rain

"No I didn't." said Wisdom not liking the accusation.

"Wisdom let's do the numbers. A 58 Corvette isn't cheap. Your guys had 72 Chevelle convertibles which will run you about $25,000 naked, add wheels; $7,000-$10,000; paint $5,000-$10,000; stereo system $12,000-$20,000; and a chromed out motor will run you $4000. There is no difference in buying a Range Rover." said Rain

"I never thought about it that way." Wisdom replied

"Most don't Wisdom but people can recognize money, especially the police." Rain emphasized.

"I got to figure out something." said Wisdom

"Did you leave all your money with them?" ask Rain "Hell no, I'm not crazy." Wisdom answered

"Then cut your losses, it's a part of doing business." Rain suggested.

"That's a lot of loss to be taking." said Wisdom

"You've already lost it because you are dealing with two reckless people. Coming to that conclusion on your own, softens the blow but greed prevents most people from doing it." Rain explained

"You don't realize how good they're eating; they're getting like 500 of the things." Wisdom explained.

"That's nothing Wisdom. I notice you always look at that sign when you come into the cell. What does it say?" ask Rain.

Wisdom looked at the sign and began to read.

- It is better to be alone, than in the wrong company.
- Tell me who your best friends are, and I will tell you who you are.
- If you run with the Wolves, you will learn how to howl, but if you associate with Eagles, you will learn how to soar to great heights.
- A mirror reflects a man's face, but what he is really like is shown by the kind of friends he chooses.
- The simple but true fact of life is that you become like those with whom you closely associate for the good and the bad.
- The less you associate with some people, the more your life will improve.
- Any time you tolerate mediocrity in others, it increases your mediocrity.
- As you grow, your associates will change. Some of your friends will not want you to go on. They will want you to stay where they are. Friends that don't help you climb will want you to crawl.
- Your friends will stretch your visions or choke your dreams.
- Those that don't increase you will eventually decrease you.

"That sign has helped me to better understand the different relationships that I find myself in, hopefully it will help you too. Know that error is the contradiction of truth. Error is a belief without understanding. Error is unreal because it's untrue. It's that which seems to be and is not. Don't make an error in not separating your friends from your associates." said Rain

"I see you schooling the youngin." said Brinks stepping into the cell.

"I'm just sharing some of the lessons that I've learned over the years. I need to run over to the canteen real quick, do either of you want anything?" asked Rain

"Naw, I'm cool." said Wisdom followed by Brinks. As Rain left the cell Wisdom was prepared to do the same but was stopped by Brinks.

"Have a seat for a minute Wisdom." Brinks requested.

"What's up Brinks?" asked Wisdom sitting back down.

"Someone whacked Rex." Brinks said while watching Wisdom's reaction.

"That's what his lying rat ass gets, he didn't see me do shit and he aint no kin to me," said Wisdom happy to hear the news.

"How is your case going?" asked Brinks

"Things seem to be moving slowly and these courts don't seem to be honoring their own law." said Wisdom.

"Yea, I've experienced that myself but you must persevere and never quit. Defeat doesn't finish a man, quitting does. A man is not finished when he's defeated, he's finished when he quits." said Brinks

"You don't have to worry about that, I'll never quit." said Wisdom.

"I never took you as someone who would." said Brinks with a proud smile on his face.

CHAPTER TWELVE

Dank's first year at Princeton was off the chain with so many different nationalities of woman, who seemed to love his southern accent. He set out to experience them all sexually. With Young Gunner scheduled to arrive soon, he hoped that he wouldn't mess up his groove.

Having Young Gunner living with him would be nice but Dank knew that Young Gunner had a lot of street in him still. He had his work cut out for him, grooming him on how to conduct himself in this new environment wasn't going to be easy.

Dank couldn't believe how hard they'd hustled in the streets to afford college and these kids were living high on the hog off their folks, none of them ever had to slang bricks or hug the block to eat.

He'd met Lisa, a Columbian and Black chick majoring in business finance while in the library studying. Quickly hitting it off, they decided to study at Dank's place instead. Lisa was hot and Dank couldn't wait to beat that pussy up. Entering his house, Dank wasted no time caressing and explore her body. Her soft ass felt like it melted between his fingers as he grabbed both cheeks and pulled her tightly against his dick.

Quickly removing Lisa's sweater and red bra revealing beautiful D cup breasts, Dank's mouth found her nipples setting off moans of pleasure. Lisa removed his pants, taking his dick into her hands and stroking it before taking his dick in and out of her mouth, letting it slide all the way to the back of her throat.

"Damn, Dank, it's so big." she said, briefly stopping to admire it before taking it back into her mouth.

"That's enough you can suck on it later, take these pants off." Dank ordered as he helping her to her feet. Lisa's pants and panties were off in one swift motion. Dank, pushed her against the wall and then pushed the head of his dick against her tight opening, her wetness allowing him to ease right in.

"A little at a time," she moaned as she eased her ass into him.

Dank began to stroke her pussy like it was the last that he would ever encounter, with a steady, slow grind that caused Lisa's body to rock against his.

"I'm cumming! I'm cumming!" she screamed as she bucked back against him. That was all it took for him to reach his nut.

Since that day Lisa and Dank had been a couple although she allowed him to sex other female as long as she was there. Dank had a thing for beautiful women and so did Lisa on occasions. This arrangement allowed both of them to feel comfortable in their relationship.

Although the house was considered family property, Dammoe and Uncle Ronnie had been the only ones to ever visit. Uncle Ronnie had been there when Dank first went off to school to make sure that he was settled in. Dammoe visited often because of all the fine rich young chicks on campus.

"I can't wait to meet your family, they sound so interesting." Lisa said as she prepared a meal for them.

"They are," said Dank not sure if she fully understood

"Are they flying in?" asks Lisa

"No they're driving, sleeper wanted to bring the new SLR. I don't know why he won't leave that hot ass car at home." Said Dank

"Dank, its summer, everyone wants to floss no matter where they are." said Lisa

"Not me and especially not out of State, jacking is a hobby around here." said Dank

"Not in this area." said Lisa

"Maybe not but Sleeper gonna want to hit the clubs in the hood." said Dank

"Yea, that may be a problem. Dudes don't know how to act sometimes." Lisa agreed

"Yea and you don't know Sleeper." said Dank

Dammoe, Sleeper, Young Gunner and Uncle Ronnie arrived at the house around 1:00pm. Pulling into the large drive, they got out of their cars.

"Damn, this how we living out here?" asked Young Gunner noticing the two story four bedroom home with the pool in the back.

"No doubt, you know how we do it." said Dammoe

"I should have moved out here sooner." said Young Gunner

"Remember Youngin you are out here to get an education. Said Uncle Ronnie

"I won't but I'm gonna enjoy this." said Young Gunner

"Why is Dank riding this F150 when everybody else ridding BMW's, Benz's and Porsche Trucks?" ask Sleeper disgusted.

"Because he's smarter then all of your dumb asses." Answered Uncle Ronnie

"He might be but I'm trading this Yukon in and getting one of those Range Rover Sports." said Young Gunner

"You are not about to bring any heat on Dank, do you understand me?" ask Uncle Ronnie stepping in close and invading Young Gunner's space.

"Uncle Ronnie look around, I won't stick out in one of those." said Young Gunner in his defense.

"You bring him any problems; I'll be to see you." Said Uncle Ronnie giving Young Gunner a look that left no mistaking that he didn't want to see him.

"Uncle Ronnie you got to enjoy life some." said Sleeper

"Money makes yall stupider, I'm flying back." said Uncle Ronnie

"Uncle Ronnie I brought the Maybach so we could travel in style and comfort." said Dammoe offended.

"Dammoe, who in their right mind buys a half million dollar car to drive themselves around, better yet, who buys a half a million dollar car and doesn't have at least ten million in cash put up?" ask Uncle Ronnie

"Uncle Ronnie we good, we eating." said Dammoe

"Yall some clowns with no makeup on. Hakim, take a good look at these two fools, they're their own victims. Their demise will be self-inflicted wounds." said Uncle Ronnie in disgust.

Dank and Lisa heard them out front and opened the front door to greet them.

"I thought you were bullshiting." said Lisa seeing the Maybach.

"I wish I was." said Dank wishing Wisdom was there because things had gotten out of control.

"Hakim, welcome home." said Dank

"Dank show me some respect, you know its Young Gunner And who is this, is she for me?" ask Young Gunner rubbing his hands together.

"Stand down, this me, meet Lisa. And it IS Hakim around here, we are trying to go without being seen. You will work at Creative Black Minds Incorporated "CBMI" and work your way up. You need to understand all aspects of the business." Dank explained to him.

"Hold up, I didn't come here to become domesticated" said Young Gunner.

"This boy is too spoiled." said Sleeper

"Boy is in the jungle looking for Tarzan" said Young Gunner feeling disrespected.

"My bad, you right." said Sleeper throwing up his hands.

"What is CBHI?" ask Hakim.

"It's our investment company." said Dank

"What do we invest in?" ask Hakim.

"Anything that doesn't go against our morals and principals." said Dank.

"Hakim, do what Dank told you." said Uncle Ronnie

"Now that's settled come on in, I made something for you to eat." said Lisa leading the way.

"Good because I'm hungry." said Dammoe

"That aint nothing new." said Sleeper
After eating later that night everyone hit the town except Uncle Ronnie who chose to watch American Greed on CNBC instead.

"So where are we off too?" ask Sleeper

"We own a piece of "Opulent" an upscale club, we'll go there answered Dank.

"Cool because you know I don't go nowhere without being heated up." said Sleeper

"There's no need for that Sleeper. Opulent is on the top two floors of a luxury building. You must have a special black card to even get in." said Dank producing the black card needed to get in.

"Where's mine?" asked Sleeper

"It ain't that easy." Dank replied.

"What do you mean, I aint good enough?" ask Sleeper heated.

"Sleeper we family but you all don't get what Uncle Ronnie has been trying to teach us, we must evolve with the times. People who are truly wealthy don't buy Roll Royce's or Maybach, yea you have your exception. Instead they buy the company so that they can sell them to those who want to appear wealthy." Dank schooled them.

"Dank, don't forget where you came from." Dammoe warned.

"Never, I love the hood but African Americans have become largely consumers indebted to other nationalities. Most African American communities remain economically underdeveloped, mired in poverty, and politically unstable. Realizing this common weakness, it is our duty to educate and organize the uplifting of African American's beginning with Kinloch." said Dank.

"You sound like Wisdom and Uncle Ronnie." said Sleeper.

"I take that as a complement. Wisdom and I talk on a regular; he breathes on me every chance he gets. Uncle Ronnie has been the glue that holds this family together. You all seem to think that he is crazy or just old and don't know anything. He's been dropping jewels on us that people would pay dearly for. Make no mistake, I'll kill a brick, make medicine sick, and drown a cup of water about all of you but you all have lost focus." said Dank rather sadly

"You've made a valid point Dank. Sleeper and I have gotten caught up in the fruits of the hustle. Thanks for painting this picture for us and bringing us back into focus." said Dammoe.

"You don't say, just a little." said Hakim taking the sting of the situation.

"That's what family do but you need an exit plan. We don't need street money anymore, we can build off what we have." said Dank.

"We're all on the same page now; I'm ready to get some of this legit money. Let's enjoy tonight, we're heading back home tomorrow." said Sleeper looking forward to a brighter future.

CHAPTER THIRTEEN

Sleeper arrived at Dammoe's penthouse at Chase Park Plaza prepared for a long night of counting money. Stepping off the elevator into the elegant living room that cost Dammoe a small fortune, Dammoe was sitting in front of three money counting machines feeding them money.

"Took you long enough." said Dammoe looking up.

"Keisha needed me to put it down, you know how that is." said Sleeper.

"Whatever, let's get this done." said Dammoe wrapping stacking of ten thousand in rubber bands.

"Don't be hating because the chicks be choosing up with me." said Sleeper with a smile.

"Hating, ha, ha, nigga you aint getting chicks because of your looks." said Dammoe

"Maybe not, but it aint tricking if you got it," said Sleeper taking a seat in front of several money counting machine.

"There are two types of tricks, those who know it and those who are in denial." said Dammoe

"I aint in denial, on another note, seems like all we do is count money these days." said Sleeper with a smile.

"Your point?" asked Dammoe

"I aint complaining, things just seem different." said Sleeper.

Things had in fact changed a lot. Dammoe and Sleeper had lost the connect Wisdom left them with because their money was always coming up short. They were use to getting bricks for $12,000 but had to turn back to Fathead. Who, in turn because of their disloyalty wanted $20,000 cash or $24,000 on consignment, this arrangement allowed them to eat but they had to work twice as hard which was taking its toll on them.

While at All Hands on Carwash, on Airport Rd, waiting to get their cars washed, a Blue drop top Ferrari with cream interior driven buy one of the finest chicks they'd ever seen pulled onto the lot; riding shotgun was the biggest blackest ugliest man they'd ever seen. Exiting the car nothing really stuck out about dude but you could tell by the greeting that he was receiving he was known and respected.

"How in the hell did his big ass fit into that car?" Sleeper was saying as Duke the owner of All Hands On stepped out to greet dude.

"Big Black, it's been a minute since I last seen you." said Duke shaking Big Black's hand.

"Been on the move, How you doing?" ask Big Black.

"Blessed, thing are good." replied Duke Most people didn't know that Big Black was the real owner of all five All Hands On carwashes and a number of other businesses which is the way he wanted it.

"That's a nice Chevelle. Whose ride is that?" asked Big Black admiring the car.

"It belongs to dude over there, they call him Dammoe. You want to meet him?" Duke was saying but Big Black was already on his way to approach Dammoe and Sleeper.

"How you doing family?" Big Black said while extending his hand to Dammoe.

"You aint no family that we know." said Sleeper getting to his feet.

"Stand down Sleeper" said Dammoe noticing for the first time the two dudes in the black Range Rover with tented windows posted up packing serious heat and the female with a noticeable burner in her hand standing up in the Ferrari

"Listen to your man, I come in peace. I noticed the Chevelle over there and was told that it belong to you. I like the car and wanted to make you an offer for it. When Duke told me who you were, I had to meet you." said Big Black flashing a friendly smile.

"Why?" ask Sleeper

"Because me and your man Wisdom are really cool." said Big Black

"He's never mentioned you." said Sleeper

"When have you ever known Wisdom to brag? He knew of me when he was out but we never did business. I got locked up for a minute on a parole violation and we got real cool in the County Jail. He spoke highly of both of you so I figured any friend of his is a friend of mine." Big Black was explaining but stop talking when the loud stereo blasting from the Audi R8 pulling up catching his attention, not because of the car but because they had a policy that prevented loud music from being played on the lot; however, he wasn't surprised to see Fathead. Jumped out once he saw Big Black he made his way over.

"Big Black what you doing talking to them?" asked Fathead letting Big Black know that they weren't on their level.

"They family." stated Big Black giving him the look.

"Why didn't yall say yall were family. I would have been throwing those thangs at yall for family prices?" asked a now leery Fathead.

"It's all good." said Big Black.

"What have you been taxing them?" asked Big Black knowing that Fathead was a greedy man·

"20?" Fathead answered.

"Dammoe, Sleeper, from here on out, yall deal directly with me. Your price is sixteen on consignment or fourteen five cash. How yall want to get down?"

"We don't take fronts, let us regroup and we'll get back to you." said Dammoe.

"Look, we family. I know yall been blowing money since Wisdom been down. I tell you what; I'll give you three bricks for the Chevelle and two bricks for 442. If you want to buy them back within 30 days for the price equivalent to what I just quoted, they're yours." said Big Black.

That was three years ago and things haven't been the same since meeting Big Black. Dude balled harder than anyone they'd ever met. He wasn't flashy like rappers or athletes but you knew he had money because of the GS, the 150 foot Yacht, or the 1959 Ferrari 250 GT LWB California Spyder that he purchased at the Pebble Beach auction for $4,455,000 which he drove as an everyday driver.

"How much are we short?" asked Sleeper not understanding how that could possibly be.

"My count is 5.4 million. So we're one hundred grand short. We are blowing too much money. There is no way we should ever be coming up short and still accepting fronts." said Dammoe disappointed.

"The fronts aint the problem and is a good thing because he going to protect his product. If we were paying cash we would be on our own to get it back. The problem is we been rolling with him trying to keep up blowing all our profits." Said Sleeper.

"Man, this shit is crazy, we've moved at least 10 tons over the last 3 years. Although we have all the material things that a man could want, we have no cash." said Dammoe disgusted with himself.

"Yea, Uncle Ronnie was right, our money ain't right." Sleeper admitted.

"We ain't spending no more money. We going to grind these next two shipments and it's a wrap." said Dammoe.

"Big Black said that he's sending us 1000 this time. We got to stack all of this from here on out. We should clear $5.5 million if we slang'em for $17,500." said Sleeper

"Naw, we taking this back to block days. Dudes are slanging quarter birds $7000 because shit is kind of tight right now. We gone hit the hoods slanging them for $5000. We'll clear $8 million then" said Dammoe

"It's going to take longer." said Sleeper.

"So, we about to cashout anyway." said Dammoe. Dammoe and Sleeper packed the money in suitcases, and then got onto the elevator heading down to the parking garage in the basement were Big Black's men waited.

Stepping off the elevator into the parking garage; after looking around making sure everything was good, they approached the waiting van. Sleeper was surprised when he opened the door and there sat Big Black coming to collect the money himself.

"Big Black, I didn't think you got your hands dirty anymore." said Sleeper smiling.

"When you get to the point that you don't want to handle your own business, you should quit." said Big Black with a serious look on his face.

Something felt odd to Dammoe but we waved it off as he put the last bag in the back of the van. Making his way around to the side of the van, he noticed Sleeper sitting in one of the seats knocked out.

Two of Big Black's men quickly grabbed Dammoe from behind, held him as one injected him with something that made him drossy. The two men then tossed Dammoe into the van and waited for Big Black to give the next instructions.

Big Black was in a daze himself thinking about Bam and Jinks his two poor excuses of nephews. They were his sister's boys, but family no less, and no one got away with messing with his family.

He'd heard that Wisdom's crew had murdered his nephews because they disrespected them by robbing one of their customers and although he knew that they had what they got coming to them, his pride wouldn't let this ride.

At the time of their deaths Big Black wasn't in a position financially to extract his revenge and get away with it, so he waited patiently studying the great warriors and generals of history while getting his money right.

Instead of killing Wisdom and his crew, Big Black saw an opportunity. His new connection was a Panamanian who was flooding him with bricks. Observing Wisdom's crew from afar, he knew that they could move them easily for him; however he just as quickly observed that his plan wouldn't work with Wisdom in the picture.

Using Captain Smith, who has been in his pocket since he was patrolling the streets to find someone to point Wisdom out as the shooter, allowed him to put his plan into affect.

Captain Smith in turn used Rex who was a convicted felon whom he'd caught with a burner and four and a half ounces hard coming out of the pool hall to finger Wisdom. After testifying and in order to cover his track, Captain Smith murdered Rex.

Big Black had become obsessed with the great thinkers he studied. He felt that Wisdom would be a worthy opponent so he arranged for himself to be locked up on purpose so that he could be next to Wisdom and provide him with the lessons that he himself had learned.

Knowing that Wisdom would be convicted, Big Black wanted to see if he was capable of using the knowledge that he had learned. It was Big Black who had tipped off his brother Snake that Wisdom was coming knowing that Wisdom would crush him.

Word had gotten back to Big Black that Snake had taken advantage of his nephew Jinks sexually when they were behind The Walls. This secret was kept from Bam who would have no doubt murdered Snake; however, Big Black wouldn't allow the deed to go unpunished.

"Where are we going?" one of Big Blacks guys asked snapping him out of his thoughts.

"The warehouse on the Westside." replied Big Black before drifting back into his thoughts.

Wisdom's attack on Snake in the chow hall only maimed him, just as Big Black hoped, killing him would've crushed their mother. That would come later once she has gone to heaven thought Big Black.

Arriving at the warehouse that Big Black used to package money that is shipped to his connect and money washer, Captain Smith was packing money into secret compartment of the church bus he used to traffic money across the country for Big Black.

"Why did you bring them here?" asked Caption Smith upon seeing Dammoe and Sleeper.

"They were getting reckless and must be disposed of." answered Big Black not appreciating being questioned.

"Big Black it was reckless of you to bring them here. What were you thinking?" ask a disgusted Captain Smith.

"I made an executive decision to do some restructuring starting with you. Your services are no longer need." said Big Black raising the 50 caliber firing a shot into Caption Smith's face and one into his chest.

"How do you want to handle these two?" asked one of Big Black henchmen stepping over Caption Smith's body.

"Decapitate Dammoe, make Sleeper watch and then suffocate Sleeper and dig his eyeballs out. Leave their bodies on the side of the highway, meet me at the spot and we'll head out." instructed Big Black hopping into the driver's seat of the church bus.

CHAPTER FOURTEEN

Wisdom had become accustomed to working out. Although his now chiseled body was inspiring, it was the relieving of stress that pushed him to workout harder as he planned his next move. Man-Man was already at the pull-up bar when Wisdom approached.

"Good Morning. What's the routine?" ask Wisdom setting his things down.

"21 pull-ups, 21 boo-yahs, that box is 25 inches jump up on it 21 times standing up each time, then do 21 sit-ups, that's one round. We'll do four rounds, set of 21, 15, 10, and 8. Then we'll get a couple of miles in." said Man-Man.

"Sounds good, let's get it in, I got to hit the shower and go to work." Said Wisdom.

Wisdom and Man-Man moved from station to station completing each exercise with ease in the beginning. Then the fourth round began, it took its toll but they pushed their way through it.

"Good job." Man-Man said as they completed the last set.

"You trying to kill me!" said Wisdom slightly sucking in air.

"Never, we go hard, that's what we do, let's get these laps in." said Man-Man before leading off at a nice pace.

Wisdom quickly caught up with Man-Man, knowing from their previous runs that Man-Man liked to run 2 miles within 15 minutes helped him to mentally set the pace for the run.

"Nice workout." said Man-Man as they came to a stop after the last lap.

"Yea, I really enjoyed it, got to hit the showers and head to work. I'll catch you later." said wisdom grabbing his water bottle and towel heading for the showers.

Wisdom had become well versed in the law since obtaining a job in the law library. Never would he have imagined that the law was so complicated and designed with so many obstructions; preventing a man from obtaining his freedom even when the law was supposedly on his side.

He quickly realized that freedom is never voluntarily given by the oppressor; it had to be demanded by the oppressed.

All aspects of the law became interesting to him once he realized how much the law affected every part of his life. He found civil law the most intriguing and lucrative. With a pen a man could bring a giant to its knees.

Wisdom was assigned to 5C lockup as the Ad-Seg law clerk. His job consisted of assisting inmates in whatever legal matters they might have, this at times was challenging to say the least.

Moving door to door seeing if legal assistance was needed, Wisdom reached George Scott door. George has been in Ad-seg 21 years, since the day he broke the Wardens jaw and pissed on him. Word is the Warden called George a boy during a conversation. George informed the Warden that boy was a racist word when direct toward a man. Ignoring George, the Warden called George a boy again and with lightning speed George hit him twice putting him to sleep before he even hit the ground, grabbing the Warden by the legs, George pulled him behind a desk where the guards found him soaked in piss.

"Need anything George?" asked Wisdom

"Naw, Wisdom I'm cool, but tell Brinks I said good looking out." George said referring to the cigarettes and coffee that Brinks made sure that he got once a week.

"Will do." said Wisdom

"How's that appeal coming along?" asked George

"They're keeping their foot on my neck. They act like I'm accused of killing someone in their family." said Wisdom half jokily.

"Wisdom never forget, the punishment that we have received was not for our unjust conduct, but designed by those who hold the gold and make the rules to determine justice and injustice, good and evil, means and ends and are seen as saviors to all but are truly devils and master manipulators in disguise." said George.

"You're right; I like that George, thanks." Wisdom was saying as he heard his name being called.

"Wisdom Jones you have a legal visit." said the guard approaching him.

"You sure?" asked Wisdom.

"Yea, you can finish this later." said the guard. A confused Wisdom exited Ad-Seg heading for the visiting room. He hadn't received a letter from his lawyers indicating they would be coming which was normal. Entering the visiting room Wisdom spotted John Rockford sitting with a woman that he didn't know.

"Wisdom, how you been?" asked Mr. Rockford standing to greet him.

"As well as expected for a man being held in a cage against his will." Wisdom replied.

"This is Alicia Taylor a private investigator that I use." said Mr. Rockford making the introduction.

"Nice to meet you Wisdom." said Alicia extending her hand.

"We'll see." said Wisdom shaking it.

"Wisdom, are you familiar with State v. Hartinelli, 972 S.W.2d 424? asked Mr. Rockford

"I've heard of it but can't place the facts right now." Wisdom admitted.

"Wisdom we are going to file a Rule 91 Habeas Corpus Petition based on Martinilli, this case deals with jury misconduct. More specifically the sheriff assigned to watch over the jury was sleeping with a juror during the trial." Mr. Rockford told him.

"How does that help me?" asked Wisdom

"Shortly after your trial, I heard rumors that one of the jurors in your case and a sheriff deputy assigned to watch them got married. I started digging around but couldn't find anything solid to support asking the court for a new trial." Mr. Rockford said allowing what he'd just said sink in.

"So what changed?" ask Wisdom becoming impatient.

"It has taken me this long because I couldn't find a marriage license or anyone to corroborate that they have been sleeping together during the trial. It kept nagging at me so I hired Mr. Taylor to do some digging. Please tell him what you found Ms. Taylor" said Mr. Rockford.

"Locating the marriage license took a lot of time because we didn't know what state they got married in. I searched every state and came up empty. I called Mr. Rockford to inform him of my finding but while doing so something crossed my mind, so I asked Mr. Rockford if he knew their nationality, he said that he thought they look Italian. I searched the marriage records in Italy and found a record of their marriage three months after your trial." said Alicia proudly.

"I had Alicia dig further. She was able to obtain affidavits from two jurors who saw the sheriff deputy leaving the jurors room early in the morning. Alicia also got their cell phones records to show that they were in constant communication during the trial." said Mr. Rockford.

"What the best strategy in dealing with this information?" asked Wisdom.

"I have a Habeas Corpus already prepared, we'll file it in the Cole Circuit Court here in town. Wisdom, I'm sure you've learned by now that the law doesn't work like most people think?" asked Mr. Rockford handing Wisdom a copy of the petition.

"Without a doubt." said Wisdom while looking over the petition.

"I want to hire a local lawyer to file this petition with me. I don't have any connections in this part of the state and don't want you to lose because of the good ole boy system." Mr. Rockford said hoping that Wisdom understood his logic.

"Sounds good to me, have you found someone?" Wisdom asked without taking his eyes off the petition.

"Yes, Gary Fisher, he's the best in this area. Mr. Rockford informed Wisdom.

"How much will it cost?" ask Wisdom

"$10,000, I want him to know we're serious." said Mr. Rockford.

"Then give him $25,000." Wisdom insisted.

"Wisdom you know that he's just making an appearance and not doing any real work?" ask Hr. Rockford.

"I don't care. Money is a tool, I'll get some more." Wisdom replied.

"Wisdom, your word has always been good but your friends haven't paid off the balance for your appeals" Mr. Rockford told him.

"What, how much I owe you?" ask a shocked Wisdom.

"$17,000" said Mr. Rockford.

"You'll have that, a new retainer, and the $25,000 for Mr. Fisher within 48 hours." Wisdom assured him. "Wisdom, don't get yourself in any trouble trying to pay me, you are too close to the door. I can cover this and you pay me when you get out." said Mr. Rockford

"Thanks Mr. Rockford, but anything in life worth having is worth paying for." said Wisdom.

"I understand, we must get going, we have a meeting with Mr. Fisher in 30 minutes." said Mr. Rockford standing.

"Nice meeting you Wisdom, good luck." said Alicia getting to her feet.

"Thank you, thanks for everything." said Wisdom whose thoughts were on the disloyalty shown by his friends. Exiting the visiting room Wisdom made a beeline straight to the payphones.

"Riiiiiiiiiing, Riiiiiilliing"

"Hello."

"You have collect call from the Jefferson City Correctional Center from: Wisdom. If you would like to accept press 1 if you would to block this call press 7.

"BEEP"

"You may begin your conversation now."

"Hello Sky, I need for you to take care of something for me." said Wisdom.

"Wisdom we need to talk." Sky said snuffling.

"What's all that noise in the background and is that Hakim I hear?" Wisdom asked confused.

"Yes, Wisdom someone murdered Dammoe and Sleeper." Sky said as tears rolled down her face.

"What, when?" asked a visibly shaken Wisdom

"Their bodies were found this morning. Wisdom they cut off Dammoe's head and plucked out Sleeper's eyes." said Sky as she began to cry even harder.

"Calm down Sky. Is Uncle Ronnie there?" ask Wisdom.

"You know Uncle Ronnie ain't leaving Kinloch unless he has too." said Sky.

"Let me speak to Hakim." said Wisdom

"Hakim, Wisdom wants to speak with you." yelled Sky.

"Sky I ask you not to call me by my government name, Hakim is dead, Young Gunner is back and they about to feel me!," said Hakim accepting the phone. "Wisdom, they did them wrong, they didn't have to do them like that." Young Gunner told him. "First and foremost, you are Hakim and you will stand down." ordered Wisdom. "Wisdom but they are family." said Hakim pleading with Wisdom to allow him to extract revenge. "They knew what they were getting themselves into Hakim. You have a long prosperous life ahead, in two years you will have a degree in business, stay focused." Wisdom pleaded with him. "Wisdom, it ain't that easy." said Hakim.

"Yes, it is, you can hang out in Atlanta with Sky for a few days until she can get everything arrange for their funerals, then it's back to school once they are laid to rest." said Wisdom.

"Dank want to holler at you." said Hakim

"Okay, remember what I just said Hakim." Wisdom said.

"Wisdom, this shit is crazy." said Dank accepting the phone from Hakim.

"I should've known you were there, I need you to stay focused. You graduate in a year and can't let anything drag you back into the streets. Keep Hakim out of trouble, you two are out. Do you understand me?" asked Wisdom in a firm tone.

"Yea, I hear you Wisdom but you want us to accept being shit on?" asked Dank angrily.

"No, I don't. I'm just asking you to trust me just as you have in the past." Wisdom replied.

"You're in prison Wisdom, serving life without parole." Dank reminded him.

"I'm aware of that Dank; please just do as I ask." said Wisdom trying to stay calm.

"We'll keep the peace Wisdom but if one of these niggas is bold enough to claim responsibility, we're going to flat line anyone who had knowledge." Dank made clear.

"I respect that." said Wisdom.

"Do you need me to do anything?" asked Dank

"Yea, I need for you liquidate some stocks and pay Mr. Rockford. He told me today that Dammoe and Sleeper hadn't been paying him." said Wisdom

"What, those niggas was getting it bro" said a shocked Dank

"Yea, that's what I heard but it is what it is." said Wisdom.

"I have Sleeper's SLR that he kept at the house near campus for when he came to visit and some jewelry that Dammoe had me holding. I could sell that and get at least half a million." said Dank.

"Don't drive the car or sell the jewelry, I want you two to just lay low. We don't know who did it or if they know about you two." said a concerned Wisdom.

"Okay, Wisdom, I'll take care of Rockford ASAP." said Dank.

"What was all the commotion about when I first called?" ask Wisdom.

"I'll let Sky tell you Wisdom but she ain't right said a disgusted Dank handing Sky the phone.

"Hello Wisdom." said Sky.

"What is Dank talking about Sky?" asked Wisdom.

"It's hard to explain." sky answered.

"If you've found someone and have moved on Sky that's cool. I appreciate and respect the loyalty that you have shown me," said Wisdom.

"I haven't found anyone Wisdom, you have a daughter, her name is Justice, and she's four years and two months old." Sky blurted out.

"You foul Sky; never would I have ever thought you of all people would deceive and deprive me in such a way." said Wisdom as his voice began to crack.

"Wisdom, I tried to tell you but the time was never right." Sky said in her defense but knew that nothing she said would be sufficient.

Not wanting to hear another word. Wisdom hung up the phone on Sky and headed to his cell. The joy of hearing that he was getting out was overshadowed by the death of his best friends. Then to find out he had a daughter he never knew about brought about feelings that he'd never experienced.

"Wisdom, let me holler at you for a minute." said Brinks causing Wisdom to stop as he past Brinks open cell door.

"Can it wait for a minute Brinks, I got a lot on my mind?" Wisdom asked returning to see what his friend and mentor wanted.

"What's wrong?" asked a concerned Brinks seeing that Wisdom had been crying.

"My lawyer came to see me today, said he found something that will get me out of here." Wisdom said

"That's great news, why are you down then?" asked Brinks not understanding.

"Mr. Rockford told me Dammoe and Sleeper never paid him all his money. So I called Sky and could hear commotion in the background, Hakim and Dank were there although they should have been at college. Sky told me that Dammoe and Sleeper had been murdered." said an emotional Wisdom.

"Do they know who did it?" ask Brinks now feeling Wisdom's pain.

"No but whoever did it cut off Dammoes head and plucked out Sleepers eyes." said Wisdom

"You know what that means?" ask Brinks

"Yea, eye for an eye." said Wisdom.

"Wisdom anger and revenge can cause you to lose sight of your objectives. There is nothing that you can do about what happened to Dammoe and Sleeper, you must stay focused on regaining your freedom." said Brinks.

"I will but that's not all. I have a daughter that I knew nothing about." said Wisdom

"That gives you all the more reason to stay focused. How much money do you need to pay those lawyers?" ask Brinks.

"I'm good Brinks, thanks for the offer." said Wisdom.

"Okay but if you find yourself in a bind, don't hesitate to holler." said Brinks as he watched Wisdom walk away from his door.

CHAPTER SIXTEEN

Three weeks had passed since Dammoe and Sleepers funerals and Sky telling Wisdom about a daughter he knew nothing about. Anger, confusion, and revenge began to consume his every thought.

"Wisdom, I've left you to your thoughts over the past few weeks, allowing you to put things into proper perspective. However, it appears that you are allowing your anger to consume you." Jamaal said closing his book.

"I was betrayed by those I loved and would have died for." said Wisdom.

"I understand but your anger is preventing you from being objective while considering things in their entirety." said Jamaal.

"Jamaal, I hear what you're saying but why wouldn't Sky tell me that I had a daughter?" said Wisdom.

"I don't know the answer to your question. Your anger prevents you from asking Sky." said Jamaal

"I don't want to speak with her." said Wisdom.

"You're being childish Wisdom, you have a daughter together, you must have an open line of communication with her." said Jamaal.

"I'll figure out something." said Wisdom.

"I want you to read this series of books Wisdom." said Jamaal handing him Blood of My Brother I-IV.

"Why would I want to read these street novel, I lived it?" asked Wisdom confused, looking at the books.

"We all lived it Wisdom but we were too caught up in the fruits of the hustle to really understand it. I've read a lot of street novels but none like these. This brother Yusuf Woods clearly writes from experience of self, others, and/or after carefully examining the pitfalls of the game." said Jamaal.

"I have other things on my mind right now." said Wisdom trying to hand them back to Jamaal who didn't accept them.

"Wisdom, a man can't allow his rage to get in the way therefore making him a weak link in a time that only the strongest chain can win. Not a physical chain, the chain of thought, which helps us maintain and prevail." said Jamaal.

"You're right, I like that." said Wisdom

"Those are Yusuf's words, not mine. Read the books." said Jamaal returning to the book he was reading.

"I will." Wisdom said opening book one of the series.

"Wisdom Jones you have mail." yelled a guard from the bars. Wisdom hopped off his bunk; seeing the large envelope from Mr. Rockford made him nervous. Freedom felt so close but he knew not to place his faith in the corrupt legal system. Next he spotted a letter from Sky which instantly angered him. Deep down inside he knew there had to be a good reason why Sky would keep his a daughter a secret from him but wasn't quite ready to forgive her.

"You okay Wisdom?" asked Jamaal.

"Yea, I'm good." said Wisdom.

Wisdom opened the letter from sky first finding several pictures of a beautiful little girl. Words couldn't express the joy and love in his eyes.

"Jamaal, this is my baby girl." said Wisdom handing him the pictures.

"Wisdom, she's beautiful, congratulation" said Jamaal.

"Thanks." said Wisdom.

"Wisdom, God's timing is never wrong. We may not agree with the season in which he reveals things but he is never late." said Jamaal.

"I hear you Jamaal but there are things that I could have done for her." said Wisdom.

"Wisdom, she looks just fine to me. You couldn't and can't take care of her better then God. Be thankful, my friend." said Jamaal.

"I never looked at it that way." Wisdom admitted.

"Most of us don't. It's only after much suffering does a man realize that he can't do it alone." said Jamaal

"But there are a lot of guys in here who are doing all day who haven't come to that conclusion." said Wisdom.

"If a man is diligent in his efforts to change while bettering himself, he will search within to find the cause of his suffering, study much to change, and apply what he has learned to all parts of his life. If they do not, they are fools, stubborn, lazy, and should be avoided at all cost." Jamaal explained.

"If everyone was as disciplined as you, we could make some serious progress." Wisdom said smiling.

"Ha-ha, it is funny how people think that inmates are disciplined. Discipline comes through liberty, you cannot consider an individual disciplined when he has been rendered as silent, a voiceless man and as immovable as a paralytic by the system. He is an individual annihilated, not disciplined."
Jamaal schooled him.

"Why do you say that?" ask Wisdom.

"In here there are so many consequences for a person's conduct. Therefore, moving without being seen is key not only for survival but maintaining the few privileges that we do have. We'll smash something but only as a last resort" said Jamaal.

"But there are consequence on the streets." said Wisdom.

"True but not like in here, the chance of getting away doesn't exist. Look around at all the cameras and rats. The only reason why some of these dudes are breathing is because dudes don't want to go on death row for killing they worthless ass." said Jamaal

"I got away with smashing Snake." said Wisdom

"Ha-ha, Brinks made that possible, you sleep on him." said Jamaal looking up at Wisdom with a smirk.

Wisdom pondered what Jamaal had just said then turned his attention to the note that accompanied the pictures.

Dear Wisdom,
You were married to the streets and nothing that I could have said or done would have changed that. We are here when you are ready to be the father and husband we need you to be.

Love you always,
Sky

"I love yall too; I'll be home in a minute."
Wisdom said to himself. Bracing himself, not knowing
what to expect from the mail Mr. Rockford sent,
Wisdom opened the envelope, noticing that there were
no legal documents enclosed just some 5 x 12 photos.

The photo of Caption Smith and Rex was the
first to catch his attention. Then the one of Dammoe,
Sleeper and Fat Head and one of Dammoe and a dude
who Wisdom couldn't remember his name.

Immediately Wisdom knew that these photos
had to come from Uncle Ronnie. He figured that
Caption Smith used Rex to lie on him. The other
photos didn't make a lot of sense to him. Why would
Dammoe and Sleeper be messing with these guys when
they have a connect so strong, he thought to himself.
He needed to find answers to these questions.

CHAPTER SEVENTEEN

"Wisdom you're going to court tomorrow, their going cut you loose. I wanted to holler at you before you go. This experience has shown you first hand aspects of the game that so many have never considered but will surely experience if they don't wake up and get out. You've enhanced your knowledge on so many levels. Combine that with your street hustle and it's a rap no matter what business you enter. You have no reason to ever consider getting back into the game, you can't, win." said Brinks looking into Wisdom's eyes as they say playing chess.

"Brinks, my chips aren't near want I need them to be but I'm going to take what I got and build an empire. I'm through with the game, this I can promise you. I do have some unfinished business that I need your help with though." said Wisdom.

"$3.5 million has been placed in a brokerage account. Rain and I will help guide you in building your empire. How else can I help you?" ask Brinks.

"Brinks, I appreciate your offer but I don't like to be in-debt to anyone. If you could just look at this picture and tell me who ole boy is, I would be grateful." said Wisdom.

"There's no debt, this is an investment. We are a part of your team and you're a part of ours, end of conversation. Now let me see that picture." said Brinks reaching out to grab the picture.

"Those two youngsters I don't know. The other guy is Duke, he's the straw man behind All Hands On Carwash and several other businesses." said Brinks

"Straw man, you telling me he doesn't own All Hands On?" asked to Wisdom confused.

"No, all that stuff belongs to his cousin Big Black." Said Brinks

"Big Black?" repeated Wisdom not believing his ears.

"Yea, you know him?" ask Brinks.

"I knew of him on the streets but never had any dealing with him. Then when I got to the county jail, he was there." said Wisdom Brinks was now looking totally confused.

"I should have put this together a long time ago." said Brinks.

"Put what together?" asked Wisdom.

"The two guys that you are accused of killing must be some kin to Big Black in some type of way. He has a big family so there is no telling, you see Snake is Big Black's brother." said Brinks.

"Why wouldn't he get at me in the county jail?" ask Wisdom.

"He is smarter then that, he knew that he couldn't crush you without there being some serious repercussions. Besides Big Black has always been good at hiding his emotions and striking only when the opportunity was right." said Brinks

"Oh, shit. I need to warn Hakim and Dank." Wisdom said jumping to his feet.

"There's no need, Big Black doesn't kill for fun. If they could link him to it, they would be whacked by now. As you can see Big Black isn't in any of the pictures, he's good like that." said Brinks

"So why would he teach me about strategy and techniques?" asked Wisdom

"When Big Black came home from the Feds you could tell that he spent his time wisely studying. He had this saying where force is necessary, it must be applied boldly, decisively and completely. But one must know the limitations of force; one must know when to blend force with a maneuver, a blow with an agreement." said Brinks.

"How well do you know Big Black'?" ask Wisdom.

"We're the same age and grew up in the same hood. We would cross paths hustling and chasing women. He's about his business, don't sleep on him." warned Brinks.

"Should I assume he has Caption Smith on the payroll?" ask Wisdom

"You can count on it." said Brinks

"He'll know that I'm out however, he doesn't know that I know he was behind all this, giving me an advantage." Wisdom pointed out

"Yea, but do you remember when Yusuf said for a good switch to work the change has to look the same as the prototype; and if it's off in any way, a real player sees right through the trick. Look for what is different about the situation?" asked Brinks.

"Yes." said Wisdom.

"He will seek you out so that he can feel you out. He's schooled you in some regards so you are useful to him, you must make him feel comfortable with leaving you alive." said Brinks.

"That's the smartest move because he has too many resources for me to find him if he doesn't want to be found." said Wisdom.

"Duke was left alive for a reason, he's a pawn. If you don't whack him or go at him, then Big Black will assume you don't know." said Brinks.

"My emotions are in check. Benjamin Franklin said "A man of tolerable abilities may work great changes, and accomplish great affairs among mankind, if he first forms a good plan, and, cutting off all amusements or other employments that would divert his attention, make the execution of that same plan his sole study and business" crushing Big Black completely is my mission." said Wisdom.

"He was right, there's something that I need for you to do for me" said Brinks.

"No, problem, name it," said Wisdom.

"I need you to hand deliver this letter to Uncle Ronnie at your earliest convenience. Please don't allow anyone to open it, it's long overdue." said Brinks handing Wisdom the letter.

"I got you." said Wisdom accepting the envelope.

"Come on, the rest of the guys have planned a getting out party for you down in Man-Man and Wink's cell." said Brinks.

Entering Man-Man and Winks cell, Wisdom could see the excitement in the eyes of all the men from his hood that he had grown to know and care about.

"Don't look so sad Wisdom, we're right behind you." said Rain.

"Yea, Man-Man is next up to bat and we need you to pave the way for him." said Jamaal.

Looking each man in the eye, Wisdom spoke "None of you have anything to worry about or want for. I know the only way to advance is to push the person ahead of you higher up the ladder and pull up the person behind you. That way you have a friend on top pulling and a friend below pushing. That's what you all have done for me, thank you. I want for you all what I want for myself, we will eat well" said Wisdom sincerely.

"That's what I'm talking about." said Big Hands

"Wisdom, it was a pleasure meeting you." said Wink.

"Wink, I appreciate everything you've done for me starting with my first day here. If I can be of assistance, let me know." said Wisdom.

"I may need you one day, thanks." said Wink.

"That goes for you too Jamaal." said Wisdom.

"You know we eating good in here so money ain't a thing. See my moms and do something meaningful with my sons is all I ask." said Jamaal.

"Consider it done." said Wisdom

They laughed and talked until lockdown was called. Everyone hug and said their goodbyes before heading to their cells. Wisdom noticed that Jamaal hadn't said much which isn't uncommon for him but something was bothering him.

"Jamaal, what's wrong?" ask Wisdom.

"Nothing is wrong Wisdom, I'm happy to see you leave this animal factory." said Jamaal.

"You've been instrumental in getting me where I am today, I'm grateful. Although I'm walking out this gate tomorrow, I'm paving a path, not closing the door. We both know with vision and a plan we can do anything. Your delay in winning your freedom hasn't been due to a lack of finance or a good team. The problem has been you didn't have anyone on the outside with the same vision but now you do." said Wisdom.

"Wisdom, what you say is true but you have some unfinished business that will occupy most of your time. I just don't want to get my hopes up, surely you understand?" ask Jamaal.

"I do and I understand that an ounce of action is worth a ton of promises or good intentions. So I won't speak on it any further," said Wisdom.

"We are here for you when you need us, good night" said Jamaal.

CHAPTER EIGHTEEN

Early the next morning Wisdom, got dressed, took care of his hygiene and said his morning prayer. Jamaal gave him enough time to get himself together before exiting his bunk and doing the same.

"Wisdom, don't forget the lessons that have come from this. Often once the oppression is over, guys forget the fight and struggle that made it possible." said Jamaal

"I won't" said Wisdom.

"Keep God first then family, Sky and Justice need you. You don't owe any of us anything and we don' t look at it that way." said Jamaal.

"Thanks, I hear and I really appreciate everything." Wisdom said.

"Wisdom Jones, you have court." said a guard standing at the gate.

"Rack 209," yelled the guard
Wisdom gave Jamaal a pound and a hug before exiting the cell.

Man-Man and Wink could be heard yelling at Wisdom, causing Wisdom to yell back. Stopping at Rain and Brinks' cell where he found them having their morning cup of coffee. No words were exchanged both raised their cups while nodding their head's. Big Hands stood at the bars as Wisdom approached.

"Take care of things out there and we will take care of things in here." said Big Hands.

"That's what it is." said Wisdom giving Big Hands a pound before exiting the walk.

Wisdom sat shackled in the back of the Sheriff's car being transferred to the Cole County Courthouse. It had been a long time since he had been outside of the prison walls, damn freedom felt good he thought.

"I ain't ever giving this shit up again." Wisdom said to himself as the car weaved through the streets.

Arriving at the courthouse Wisdom spotted Mr. Rockford with someone he didn't recognize in front of the courthouse talking. Pulling around back, the sheriff's took him in through the side door, placing him into a holding cell. Before he could be seated, Mr. Rockford was at the door.

"Wisdom, this is Mr. Fisher, he's been instrumental in getting your case in front of a good judge and fast tracked." Mr. Rockford explained.

"Thanks, nice to meet you Mr. Fisher" said Wisdom extending his hand

"Likewise" said Mr. Fisher accepting it.

"So what's going to happen today?" asked Wisdom.

"I'll let Mr. Fisher explain." said Mr. Rockford

"We have a dead-bang winner with this jury misconduct issue, there's no way around it. The judge is by the book, he isn't scared to overturn a conviction if the law calls for it. We anticipate that he will grant you a new trial today. The state may appeal, but we'll ask for a bond, and the judge will grant it," said Mr. Fisher.

"With Rex being dead, they don't have a case. They offered you 15 years on murder two. I told them I would relay it to you." said Mr. Rockford.

"I ain't snatching shit." said Wisdom

"I thought you would say that." said Mr. Rockford.

"Gentleman court is about to begin." said the bailiff through the open door.

Sky and Uncle Ronnie sat in the front row. Sky looked beautiful as ever while Uncle Ronnie looked good as well and in great shape to be 60 years old.

Wisdom took his seat between Mr. Rockford and Mr. Fisher. Presiding was the Honorable Judge Anthony Longhorn who looked more like a clansmen then a Judge thought Wisdom.

Gentlemen, we are not going to waste a lot of the courts time on this morning. I've read over the defense's petition and the states response. Mr. Walters, you represent the attorney general's office on behalf of State of Missouri.

"What is your position?" ask Judge Longhorn

"Your Honor, our position is that there may have been juror misconduct but Mr. Jones can't show how it prejudiced him." said Mr. Walters

"Mr. Walters, I said that we wouldn't waste the courts time. You went to law school, therefore you know that this is a structural error and Mr. Jones doesn't have to show prejudice. I haven't heard you contest the affidavits as not being authentic." said Judge Longhorn impatiently.

"Judge, we've spoken to the affiant's. The State concedes that the affidavits are genuine." said Mr. Walters

"Mr. Rockford, what is your position?" ask Judge Longhorn.

"Our position is that a manifest injustice has occurred and Mr. Jones should be released immediately. The state's case was weak from the beginning supported by the lies of one alleged eyewitness. This witness your honor is no longer living, the state doesn't have a case." stated Mr. Rockford

"Is this true Mr. Walters?" ask Judge Longhorn

"Yes, your honor it is true but the state is looking for more eyewitness as we speak." said Mr. Walters.

"Your Honor Mr. Jones has been incarcerated over four years for a crime he didn't commit. The state brought its strongest case when they took Mr. Jones to trial. This Court shouldn't allow the State to use such stall tactics to keep Mr. Jones incarcerated away from his loving family." Mr. Rockford argued.

"I've heard enough. Based on the record before this Court and the concession made by the State of Missouri. I am ordering that Mr. Jones be giving a new trial within 30 days of this order. I'm further setting bail in the amount of $500,000 cash only however, Mr. Jones will be placed on house arrest. The State has the right to appeal this losing cause, something this Court frowns upon." said Judge Longhorn looking over at Mr. Walters.

"Your Honor, I have a cashier's check in the amount of $500,000 made payable to the Clerk of the Court. The Clerk indicated that the house arrest monitoring specialist is prepared to install the unit at the home of Ms. Sky Gates in Chesterfield, Missouri today." said Mr. Rockford.

"Clerk, please process the check and release Mr. Jones to the custody of Mr. Rockford. Mr. Jones, breaking the terms of house arrest and/or failing to appear for court will result in the forfeiture of the $500,000 and a warrant will issue for your arrest. Do you understand?" Judge Longhorn asked Wisdom.

"Yes, sir." said wisdom

"It is so ordered. Court is dismissed." said Judge Longhorn.

"How long is this going to take?" ask Wisdom

"About 15 minutes." said Mr. Fisher

"Good because I'm ready to get the hell out of here. Do I owe you anything Mr. Fisher?" ask Wisdom

"No, serious referrals would be appreciated." said Mr. Fisher.

"John you had a stack of cashier's checks, where did they come from?" ask Wisdom

"Sky," said Mr. Rockford

"Do you have any left?" ask Wisdom

"Sure she brought a million dollars." said Mr. Rockford.

"Please give Mr. Fisher $100,000 as a retainer for Jamaal Burns and give the rest back to Sky." Wisdom instructed.

Mr. Rockford reached into his jacket pocket, removing a cashier's check in the amount of $100,000 placing it into Mr. Fisher's hands.

"Mr. Fisher, Jamaal Burns freedom has now become your responsibility, money is no object. Clearly I understand that these things take time and planning, I won't get in your way however know that all of my resources are at your disposal, please contact Mr. Rockford if you need them." said Wisdom

"Wisdom, you've experienced my work. I'm not big on talking, silence makes no mistakes". Mr. Burns is in good hands." Mr. Fisher assured him.

"I have no doubts." said Wisdom knowing that he would orchestrate Jamaal's freedom no matter what it took.

"Gentleman we need to get Mr. Jones processed out." said the Sheriff Deputy.

Walking to the back to be processed out, Wisdom thought about all the things that he had went though. His suffering was self-inflicted wounds, with no one to blame but himself. It saddened him to think about Dammoe and Sleeper. He smiled at the thought of Dank and Hakim's success; however it was the thought of Justice that overjoyed him.

Seeing Sky brought back strong feeling and made him realize she only did what was best for their daughter.

Then there was Uncle Ronnie, something was different about him but Wisdom just couldn't put his figure on it at the moment.

"Wisdom Jones, you are free to go." said the Sheriff Deputy bringing Wisdom out of his thought. Sky ran into Wisdom arms as he exited that courthouse.

"I'm sorry Wisdom if I did anything to hurt you, I was just protecting our family." said Sky

"No I owe you an apology, in my heart I already knew that but my emotions got the best of me," said Wisdom.

"I love you Wisdom," Sky said locked in his embrace.

"I love you too; now let's go see my daughter." Wisdom said but not wanting to let her go.

"Wisdom you must go straight home, the house arrest monitor guy will be there waiting on you." said Mr. Fisher.

"You don't have to worry; I'll make sure he gets there." Uncle Ronnie assured him.

"Wisdom, let me speak to you a moment." said Mr. Rockford pulling him to the side.

"What's up?" asked Wisdom.

"Wisdom no illusion is more crucial than the illusion that success in beating the system and huge amounts of money buys you immunity from all the ill will of mankind. You are blessed to be free, don't squander this opportunity." said Mr. Rockford .

"I won't." said Wisdom.

Hoping into the passenger seat of the truck, Sky pulled off. Thinking he'd forgotten something, Wisdom searched his body and the reached into the bag containing his legal work, retrieving the letter that Brinks had given him for Uncle Ronnie.

"This is from Brinks." Wisdom said turning to hand Uncle Ronnie the letter.

Accepting the letter Uncle Ronnie looking at it for a moment considering if he should read it, before ripping it open and began to read it.

Stay tuned for the sequel:

MISEDUCATION OF A HUSTLER II:
Educated Decisions

Wisdom wants revenge for the deaths of his brothers. Years spent inside of a cage has taught him self-discipline, patience, the art of strategy and most importantly: his life could be lost forever if he makes a mistake. He vows never to allow that to happen again.

Miseducation of a Hustler II: Educated Decisions unfolds into a war of the minds. The overwhelming desire to crush those responsible for the deaths of his brothers tests all that he has learned. Witness the dangerous moves that are made to achieve success.

What do you think the letter to Uncle Ronnie said? Please join the discussion and leave your feedback.
Follow us - www.Flagrantpublishing.com
Authorjabar@wordpress.com and Authorjabar@facebook.com

Pick up your copy TODAY at Amazon.com

Good to the Last Drop

18 orgasmic original short stories that are sure to please, this tantalizing page turner is jam packed with over 200 pages that invoke the allure of 50 Shades of Grey combined with the sensuality of Zane to keep you coming back for more. Pick up your copy **TODAY!!** at Amazon.com

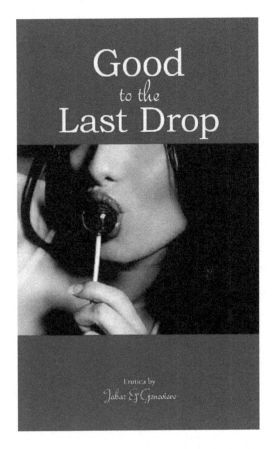